About the Author

After raising three boys in the suburbs of Chicago, Carrie Jo Howe now lives in Key West, Florida with her husband and her dog. Her new book, *Island Life Sentence*, is a fictional account of an American Midwestern woman who feels like an alien in the "one human family" of Key West. Carrie Jo's first book, *Motherhood is NOT for Babies*, received rave reviews, and works wonderfully as an alternate form of contraception. Her blog *Florida Keys Crime Report* tells of all the goings-on in the Keys, where bank robbers get away on bicycles, and perps caught with an undersized, pinched, out-of-season lobster get more jail time than drug runners. She is currently working on her second Key West book.

ISLAND LIFE SENTENCE

ISLAND LIFE SENTENCE

CARRIE JO HOWE

Unbound

This edition first published in 2018

Unbound

6th Floor Mutual House, 70 Conduit Street, London W1S 2GF

www.unbound.com

ISBN (eBook): 978-1911586531

ISBN (Paperback): 978-1911586524

Design by Mecob

Cover image:

© Shutterstock.com

Printed in Great Britain by Clays Ltd, Elcograf S.p.A.

Dear Reader,

The book you are holding came about in a rather different way to most others. It was funded directly by readers through a new website: Unbound.

Unbound is the creation of three writers. We started the company because we believed there had to be a better deal for both writers and readers. On the Unbound website, authors share the ideas for the books they want to write directly with readers. If enough of you support the book by pledging for it in advance, we produce a beautifully bound special subscribers' edition and distribute a regular edition and e-book wherever books are sold, in shops and online.

This new way of publishing is actually a very old idea (Samuel Johnson funded his dictionary this way). We're just using the internet to build each writer a network of patrons. Here, at the back of this book, you'll find the names of all the people who made it happen.

Publishing in this way means readers are no longer just passive consumers of the books they buy, and authors are free to write the books they really want. They get a much fairer return too – half the profits their books generate, rather than a tiny percentage of the cover price.

If you're not yet a subscriber, we hope that you'll want to join our publishing revolution and have your name listed in one of our books in the future. To get you started, here is a £5 discount on your first pledge. Just visit unbound.com, make your pledge and type KEYWEST18 in the promo code box when you check out.

Thank you for your support,

Dan, Justin and John
Founders, Unbound

Super Patrons

Bryan Armalavage
Ken Beadling
Roger Bottum
Anne Bouchard
Mike & Ellen Caron
Susie Cassidy
Janet Clark
Auntie B Cooper
Robert & Donna Cooper
Curt Cooper
Laurie Davies
Hal Dewsnap
Teri Foster
Nancy Gage
Jody Gordon
Donna Gustin
Jeffrey Howe
Justin Howe
Thomas Howe
Steven Howe
Marilou Howell
Melissa Jones
Christi Kapp
Ray Kennedy
Anne & Mike Kennedy
Bridget Kennedy
Mary Kennedy
Dan Kieran
Kathleen Kiser
Karen Loftus
Julie Loftus
Lawrence Looby

Lynn Looby
Ken & Jodi MacDonald
Lisa Mahoney
John A C McGowan
Debbie Merion
John Mitchinson
Vicki Mordell
Kathryn Nelson
Lisa Nevins
Gayann Pfeiffer
Justin Pollard
Anne Roberts
Sue Seboda
Peter & Sally Shapiro
Jane Soderberg
Carolyn Standlee
Cynthia Steinbach
Patty Trindl
Catherine Wilk
Susan Yeschek
June Yoshimura

With grateful thanks to Anne Bouchard, who helped to make this book happen.

Contents

Current Atmospheric Conditions

"Sunshine state... my soggy ass."

It was dark. The power and the air conditioning had gone out hours ago. Peg hugged her dog under the makeshift bed-tent, clutching him to her sweaty pajama'd breasts. An engraved locket pinned to Nipper's blue life vest dangled under his pirate dog collar. Hurricane rain pummeled the bedroom window – the violent wind shook the glass panes. Peg wondered about the moaning sound until she realized it was coming from her own throat.

She shrieked at the sudden crash on the metal roof. Several days of binge drinking without proper oral hygiene, or any hygiene for that matter, produced noxious vapors in the tent. Nipper's nostrils flared as he took in the odors and licked her fluorescent orange, cheesy, tear-stained fingers.

The teepee bedspread crushed Peg's hair into a bozo coif. Sitting on her knees, she released her grip on Nipper and reached over her head to hold up the blanket with the end of the flashlight. The beam of light cut through the darkness, jumping across the sparkling jewelry strewn in a heap on the crumpled, food-stained sheets. With her other hand, Peg lifted one long gold necklace from the tangled jewels. She sniffled as she placed the shiny strand over the dog's neck. Nipper yawned wide in anxious anticipation.

She put the flashlight in her armpit and squeezed the dog tightly. More sounds of destruction echoed down the hallway from the living room, reactivating her shivers. The booze and chips from yesterday gurgled in her stomach. Nipper cowered, squinting his eyes, ears flat to his head.

Do not throw up. Get a grip.

Snuggling him close, she yelled over the din, "Oh, my friend, you'll be okay." The dog's loving brown eyes made her heart constrict. She tightened the straps of his life jacket.

"I'll see you in the afterlife." She kissed his forehead. "Ummm, actually, I don't want to worry you, but I'll more than likely be in hell… since I'm personally responsible for the hurricane. And you know Sister Gabriel and the Catholic Church are not going to go easy on that."

Nipper blinked.

A thunderous WHAM shook the wall – a barrage of debris thrashed the house mercilessly. Gasping, Peg wet her lips with her dry tongue.

"I mean, honestly, how different can it be from here?"

Drunk Deal

FIVE MONTHS EARLIER

Peg and Clark Savage snuggled next to each other on the couch, the '80s music of their youth blasting from the stereo. Happy hour rolled through dinner hour, then seamlessly transitioned into late-night cocktails. Flames from the fireplace reflected serpent tongue shapes against the empty wine bottles lined up on the hearth.

"Oh, Clark, I love them. They're gorgeous." Peg removed the emerald heart earrings from the box and kissed her husband.

"For the smartest and most beautiful woman in the whole... wide... let me see... neighborhood." Clark laughed. His smooth hands slipped the delicate earrings through her earlobes. The green stones contrasted with her pale white skin.

Peg giggled. "Gee, you really think I'm the most beautiful woman in the entire neighborhood? Even Brabra... Barbara? She has new boobs."

"You are more ravishing now than when I met you. You know I'm a sucker for a redhead." Clark kissed the freckles on her nose. He was a smooth talker all right.

Hoping that the praise was for him, Nipper looked up, nose twitching. Realizing it was a false alarm, the copper-colored bird-dog flapped his ears and settled down again in front of the fire.

"I color my hair, you know." Peg waved her hand in a circular motion around the top of her curly ginger locks.

Clark smiled as he reached for her stockinged feet. "Wouldn't it be great to have an amazing adventure now that the business is sold? We've done our job. The FOR SALE sign is in the front yard. Once the house sells, the world is our oyster. We can live anywhere." He massaged her arches. Peg melted.

"I thought that our *anywhere* was downtown Chicago in a high-rise." She tipped her head back and sighed. "You know, restaurants, bars, opera, symphony, Cubs games – they're gonna win it all again this year, you know."

"Spoken like a true Cubs fan." He stopped rubbing her feet and said in a business-like tone, "Yes – downtown Chicago would have been great if we had to stay in Illinois. But that has changed. Illinois is bankrupt. Property taxes are going up. I can't take this weather anymore."

He softened and took her palm, tracing the pink lines with his index finger. "Think of the fun stuff we could do in Key West."

"Oh, Clark, not the Key West idea again." Peg pleaded.

"Listen to me for a minute." He very deliberately put his wine glass on the coffee table, took her by the shoulders and gazed into her pale green eyes. "There's music, and warm water and palm trees – think of it, our nights would be margaritas and long walks on the beach. We could get a boat."

A boat?

Peg felt seasick at the thought of it.

Clark got up to refill her green wine goblet. On his return to the couch, he took out a Key West brochure from inside his briefcase. The Italian red sloshed onto the glossy paper, making the tourists in the photo look like murder victims.

"You really are serious about a move to Key West." Peg surreptitiously rubbed her chin, hoping not to find that one wild hair that refused to be tamed. "But I don't know anyone in Key West. We've lived in this house for 20 years. I have my friends and community. I've never lived in a different state." She had to admit, it did sound dreamy – just the two of them, alone on a tropical island – so romantic. But then again, she was drunk.

"You can meet new friends. Change is good. Your old friends can come and visit you." Clark was in full sales mode now – face flushed, muscles bulging, hair all tousled. Peg struggled not to succumb to his powers.

"It's so far away." Peg pointed at the picture in the brochure. "On the map it doesn't look like there's land, only water... blue everywhere."

Clark was preparing his rebuttal when she blurted, "And I'm afraid of driving on long bridges. No way. Can't breathe."

"What? Since when?"

"Since 9/11."

"Oh, because there were so many bridge deaths on 9/11?" Peg backed away. Clark brought her back to him gently. "You should be afraid of living in a high-rise in the city, not bridges connecting us to paradise." He nibbled the emerald earrings on her earlobes. "Mmm, I do have good taste."

Peg resisted, annoyed that he was making sense *and* kissing her at the same time. "It's irrational, I know. I read about it. Stems from a fear of being trapped. I'd have no way to get off the island."

"The airport has jets that fly in and out all day. You're only a plane ride away."

Clark crooned seductively into her ear.

"How about that hurricane problem? What happens in that case? How do Nipper and I get out of there?" Peg took a big gulp from her glass.

Nipper opened his eyes when he heard his name. Since there was no possibility of food, ball, or squirrel, he returned to his slumber.

"I'll be there. I'll take care of you. There's always plenty of warning before a hurricane. Key West hasn't been hit by a hurricane since Wilma in 2005. Even then, no one died."

Peg's eyebrows raised at the word *died*.

"I'll be able to get you and Nipper to safety." Clark scooped up her legs and swiveled her torso until she was sitting in his lap.

Uh-oh. He really wants this. He is so irresistible. He smells like soap and campfire.

She had a vague sense of déjà vu. It had been a night like this when Clark wanted to liquidate all of their assets to buy a small Internet company; another similar evening when Clark wanted Peg to work as Chief Financial Officer; and another yet when he brought home a puppy – the best inebriated agreement by far.

"Let's go and take a look at properties. We don't have to buy anything if we don't love it. You can run the numbers to see if it makes sense financially." Clark pressed his mouth to her wrist, moving slowly up her forearm toward the inner elbow. "Such beautiful soft skin."

That whispery, sexy voice…

Peg cursed the butterflies that flitted their way through her bloodstream. She swilled the last of the liquid courage. "You know I can't resist spreadsheets." She smiled and Eskimo-kissed his nose. "Oh, okay, fine."

"That's my girl." In one swift move, Clark dumped her body off his and grabbed a wet paper towel from the table and a pen from his computer case. "Let's sign this agreement on this official document. *I, Peg, and I, Clark, agree to have an open mind while looking for properties in Key West.*" He grinned drunkenly as he signed the paper and handed it to Peg. The room was spinning as she smudged her signature next to his.

The next day, when Clark greeted Peg in the kitchen, his face lit up with hungover happiness. Peg held up the still-damp paper towel contract – black ink sticking to her index finger and thumb.

"Yes, here's the proof." She dropped the drunken pact into the desk drawer on top of the crusty remains of past contracts that refused to lie flat. She could just make out the blotchy inked words *company, job* and *dog* on the corners of the stacked agreements.

"It'll be fun, an adventure." Clark kissed her lips, his breath a mixture of mouthwash and sour bar towel. "I'll make the arrangements. We can get away at the end of the week."

Peg wished that he would stop saying the word *adventure*.

Narrowly, Keeping an Open Mind

"No direct flights from Chicago? Not even on a different day of the week?" Peg checked her seat belt and memorized the safety instruction card in the seat pocket as the plane engines kicked into full gear.

"One longer flight to Miami and then a short hop to Key West. It's faster than driving back home from O'Hare during rush hour." Clark could hardly contain his excitement.

The gray gloom of chilly Chicago clouds slowly turned to puffy white floaters as they journeyed south. Clark fanned out the real-estate fact sheets on the tray table and pointed to the yellow highlights on the page. "This house looks good. It would be fun to have a pool."

"It does look shimmery and the palm trees are beautiful." She hugged Clark's arm.

It's nice to see him so happy.

After much discussion about the pros and cons of each property, Peg ranked the house sheets based on affordability and amenities and stacked the papers neatly. The flight attendant walked the aisle to check seat belts as the plane started its descent. Peg sucked in her stomach and pointed to the latched belt.

"Like this is really going to save us from a fiery crash at 400 miles per hour." She clutched Clark's knee.

"Safer than driving a car, Peg." Clark patted her hand and stared out of the airplane window.

Hmm, maybe, but what about driving a car on a bridge?

Miami International Airport was bustling with travelers. The short skirts and stiletto heels were a far cry from the layered coats and heavy boots of three hours ago.

"I need a coffee." Peg rubbed the sleepies out of her eyes. "Where should I meet you?"

Clark checked the flight info board. "Key West – leaves from D60."

"Okay, I'll meet you there." Peg wandered up and down the terminal for a sign or a symbol of a coffee cup. She walked up to an official-looking man. "Excuse me. Is there a Starbucks around here?"

The man looked at her quizzically.

"Starbucks?" Peg repeated. "Coffee?" She mimed a coffee-drinking motion, complete with blowing on her hand shaped like a cup.

"Ahhhh. Starbooks. No." He shook his head. "Cafe. Si, Senora." He pointed past several gates to a bakery.

Peg thanked him and took her place in the long line of stylish women, businessmen, large families and NO ENGLISH. Both customers and shopkeepers were relaxed as they bantered about God-knows-what.

The man in front of her asked for *something*.

The salesgirl nodded and delivered *something*.

Peg wondered if it was the same *something* that she wanted.

She cursed herself for not paying better attention when the *something* had changed hands.

She read the menu posted above the workers.

What is this stuff? Ajiaco? Medianoche? Cortadito?

Peg's coat and scarf started to create extra heat as she got closer to the counter. With each step forward she became more anxious. She just wanted coffee, milk, no sugar.

Why didn't I take Spanish instead of French? I had a choice in fifth grade, but nooo, that cute boy in the neighborhood took French. Ugh, I was such a follower, if only I had–

"Senora?"

It was her turn.

Beads of sweat formed around her temples. The salesgirl looked at her expectantly. Peg pointed at an item on the board that looked like it could have possibly been a cup of coffee. The woman acknowledged the request, turned to the coffee maker and worked feverishly at the beverage.

Okay, good sign.

Having finished her creation, she handed Peg the drink.

I must have asked for the itty, bitty smallio.

The tiniest of tiny cups held the blackest and darkest of liquid – thicker than tar, yet smelling the same. Holding the styrofoam thimble between her thumb and forefinger, she took a sip.

Yechhh.

She scraped her tongue against her teeth and made a face. The flavor and texture reminded her of her youth, when she had lost a bet and had to lick the neighborhood swing set.

She tossed the miniature cup of poison in the garbage can before descending on the escalator to gate D60. Walking off of the bottom step, she plunged into the alternate universe of gates in the basement of Miami International Airport.

Twelve gate agents in close proximity announced 12 flight numbers, in multiple languages, to a sea of humanity. A family with five children jostled their way toward the Costa Rica flight, next to the three-piece-suited businessman trying to get to Huntsville, Alabama, next to the boozy tourists hooting and hollering in the line for the flight to Key West.

Peg scanned the crowd to find Clark.

My God. This is like a bus station… with wings.

She located him in a corner seat wedged between Santa Claus in a brightly colored floral shirt and a woman with a slobbery 100-pound pit bull service dog.

Clark was laughing while talking on the phone. He hung up when he saw Peg. "Where's your coffee? Did you get me one?" He yawned.

"No, but now I seriously wish that I'd gone for a mojito at the bar upstairs before coming down here. What *is* this place, anyway?" Peg's head spun as her eyes darted right and left. "Who was on the phone?"

"Business stuff." Clark stretched his arms and legs casually.

She plopped her now unnecessary outerwear on the floor next to him. "What kind of business stuff? We don't own a business anymore."

Clark cocked his head and held up a hand. "Did she say final boarding to Key West?" He jumped up and saw the gate agent ready to close the door. "That's our flight. Let's go." He yanked up his backpack and motioned for Peg to follow.

Peg scooped up her belongings and bumped her way through the crowd. "I'm coming." She shifted the coats to one arm and gave the agent her ticket with her free hand. Scurrying behind Clark in an outdoor hallway, she climbed up the long metal ramp into the plane.

"Only 30 seats on this plane?" Peg grabbed Clark's arm and spoke into his ear. "Propellers? What year was this plane made, 1914? My seat is right behind the pilot. Who looks like he's six years old, by the way," she whispered as they sat down.

Clark gave her hand a double pat, then closed his eyes and promptly fell asleep as the plane took off.

Peg removed the airline magazine from the seat pocket in front of her. The sudoku and numbrix had been completed by a previous passenger. The magazine in front of Clark's seat was sealed shut with a sticky piece of chewed gum. She sighed and placed her forehead against the plane window to look down at the islands below.

So bright… blindingly bright.

Fine lines of white connected the tiny puzzle pieces of land in the middle of endless blue. Closing the window shade with clammy hands, her stomach sickened.

Those are miles and miles of bridges. Never ending, limitless. Trapped. No way out.

She moved closer to Clark, who had started to drool. She closed her eyes.

I must be strong. I can do this.

The self-flagellation came to a premature halt as Kindergarten Captain announced the imminent landing. "Ladies and gentlemen, I just want to tell y'all that this's gonna be a quick landing. I'm a Navy-trained pilot and I can do this with my eyes closed," the pilot showboated, "but today, I'll keep 'em open. Runway's pretty short – makes it kinda fun."

Peg gripped the armrest and elbowed Clark. "Wake up. The pilot said…"

With a fast descent, big bounce and screeching brakes, they touched down on the tiny runway in Key West. The passengers whooped a drunken *hooray*. Peg re-swallowed the food from that morning's breakfast.

She stepped down the narrow metal airplane stairs onto the tarmac. "Don't they have jetways? What happens if it rains?" Peg yelled to Clark through the engine noise on the tarmac. "Might be possible to get sucked into a propeller. Not safe."

Kind of like a third world country.

"It's always beautiful here. It never rains. Doesn't this tropical air feel amazing?" Clark yelled back with his arms in the air.

Peg noticed a group of gigantic lifelike mannequins on the airport roof, arms opened wide: WELCOME TO THE CONCH REPUBLIC, the sign read. The looming figures looked weather-beaten and tired.

Seriously hoping that this is not prophetic.

At the one and only airport gate, the realtor met them with bottles of water and a pile of listing sheets. Crossing the parking lot, Peg realized she was overdressed in her white belted Burberry jacket and Italian Aquatalia leather boots. The sun seared through her scalp. The arch of armpit moisture grew larger. Her hair immediately expanded to an afro that rivaled the likes of a young Michael Jackson.

She glanced at her reflection in the window through fogged sunglasses.

Socks and boots? What was I thinking?

Her feet swelled like dim sum in their leathery incarceration.

The real-estate hunt slogged at first. The houses were turn of the century, with clusters of chopped-up rooms, bang-your-head ceilings, and closets instead of basements and garages. Most places didn't have laundry facilities and, if they did, the machines were located outside of the house, under a lean-to, in the yard. With no driveways, and a general lack of available parking, the car would be able to do lots of sightseeing as it made its daily move to different spaces on the dusty city streets.

Clark looked at outdoor space – for his outdoor lifestyle. Peg looked at indoor space – or lack thereof.

As they toured another underwhelming property, Peg shook her head, "Ugh. Like the other houses we've seen, this master bedroom won't fit any of our furniture." She was getting discouraged.

Clark was not to be deterred. "We'll be living outside mostly."

"Our *bed* will not be outside." Peg's hairs at her neckline were clumped in a wet, kinky roll.

After inspecting eight disappointing, doll-sized houses, some that looked like they kept a century of termites very happy, the three of them were ready to call it a day. Walking to the car, Peg saw a real-estate listing sheet on the ground. The wind suddenly picked up, and the paper blew round and round until it settled against Peg's leg. Her neck sweat chilled in the breeze and she shivered.

"Here, you dropped this." Peg handed the sheet to the realtor.

"Hmm. It's not mine... weird. I didn't know this house was on the market. It's been vacant for a couple of years. I always wondered why, 'cause it's a great house. And it's right across the street. I'll see if we can get in." The realtor pointed to a house on the other side of the intersection. She glanced at the listing sheet and dialed her phone.

Peg and Clark followed behind her as she walked and made arrangements.

"Good news. We're in luck. We can look at it now." The realtor led the way to the house, up the porch steps, to an unlocked front door. "Hmm, apparently the seller isn't worried about break-ins. Funny there's no lock-box. Never seen that before. Oh well, let's go in."

Peg shook off a shudder as she entered the house. "Whoo, I must be dehydrated."

The realtor called the house a Key West Conch. "It was built in the early 1900s on the other side of the island. At some point it was lifted off the ground and carried by mules to this location. No one knows exactly when or by who. One of the many Key West mysteries." She laughed and game-show-hosted the room with a flat hand. "The floors and walls are Dade County Pine, although the walls are whitewashed, giving it more color and texture. This wood is nearly extinct now."

Peg noticed the striping of dark brown and burgundy at her feet. "Wow, a lot of trees sacrificed their lives for this house. I hope they're not still mad," she joked while caressing the grainy wall. A tiny splinter wedged its way into her thumb. "Ouch." Narrowing her eyes at the seemingly innocent walls, she followed Clark and the realtor out of the large white back door.

"The deck is made out of Brazilian Ipe wood – one of the heartiest woods available. It's naturally resistant to rot and decay – and bugs." She laughed. "We got a few of those down here."

The yard was overgrown with a variety of lush palms interspersed with alien-shaped flowers. "Hey, is this a baby lime tree?" Peg picked up a tiny green ball from the rocky ground.

"Yes, your very own Key Lime tree." The realtor checked her phone as she spoke.

"That's cool. I don't think we could grow one of these in Chicago." Peg smiled. As if on cue, the Caribbean breeze whistled around the yard.

"Margaritas in our own backyard." Clark grinned from ear to ear and said, "Oh yes. Yes. Ohh yes. All of the Key West charm – old but renovated. Small but open floor plan. Yeah baby. Gated yard. Ohh yes."

He was, quite possibly, orgasmic.

He looked to Peg for confirmation. "We could afford this right? After the house is sold? You'll do the numbers?"

The realtor looked up from her phone. "The sellers are motivated, they'll negotiate."

Peg turned away from him to gaze at the picture windows overlooking the swaying palm trees. Sunshine beamed throughout the room – like heaven itself had opened up its portals.

Yes, this was the house. She did the math in her head. Even at list price, it was doable. Seeing the rapture in her husband's face, she realized that they were, in fact, going to relocate to Key West, Florida.

The Savages were moving to the island.

The Walk and Talk

After the house-hunting trip, back in her Illinois home of 20 years, Peg looked around the kitchen. She soaked in that *feeling of familiar* – the table leg chewed by Nipper when he was a puppy, the window that refused to lock, the mysterious dent in the refrigerator door.

Sighing, she turned her attention to the dog. "Ready to go for a walk, Nip?"

Nipper crouched by the side door, gnawing on his footpad. The leash hung on the knob. Peg shoved her size eights into the minus-100-degree-rated boots while double-zipping the thermotech coat, topping herself off with a black fur Cossack hat.

Clark sat at the kitchen counter, his head buried in his computer. "Ahhh, the month of March in the Midwest."

Before Peg could retort, the 50-pound vizsla barreled through her puffy legs and out the door. "Okay, okay, I guess you *do* want to go for a walk today."

Once in the car, Peg could see the dog's beany brown eyes staring at her in the rearview mirror as she backed out of the garage. "What d'you think? Are we brave enough to make a big move like this?" Nipper cocked his head to one side then sat back in the seat to resume chewing on his footpad. In solidarity, Peg bit a hangnail off her thumb as she left the driveway.

Noticing the FOR SALE sign had blown across the front yard, Peg hit the brakes and got out of the car. Slipping on the icy ground, she wiped off the muddy sign and rehung it on its windy perch. Ever since they bought the house all those years ago, she thought the house looked like a surprised cartoon character. The top two windows opened wide-eyed, and the oval door gave the lip-like impression of someone getting goosed from behind. As she replaced the sign, she looked up at the windows. Icicles had formed tears under the shutters.

"You are *not* going to make me cry, Mr. House," she said as she climbed back into the car. "But thank you for reminding me that I need to schedule Clark's colonoscopy."

Nipper wagged his tail, licked her face and whined with dog-joy at her return.

Waving to Trudy from across the brown slush of the field, Peg navigated around the dog, remnants of winter oozing from the ground. Trudy's fluorescent purple coat obscured most of her frame. Her short hair spiked over the multicolored headband that covered her forehead and the top of her horn-rimmed glasses.

Peg and Trudy had stomped across this 40-acre dog park every day for the past 16 years. They remembered past discussions by the various geographic anomalies in the terrain. The flooded pond – the death of past dogs. The sinkhole in the middle of the field – the slutty neighbor who flirted with all of the husbands. The rotting tree stump – male brain deficiencies.

"Hi. Oh, watch out, be careful," Peg warned her friend as Trudy's Labrador, Tucker, bounded up to them. From the looks of Trudy's backside, Tuck had already accomplished one back-of-the-knee body slam today. Trudy rubbed her rump and threw her hands in the air with a look of exasperation.

"I know. So much for the thousand-dollar dog training."

As they started on their trek, the dogs took off after a rabbit. They hurtled across the wet meadow, back feet surpassing front feet with cheetah-like speed.

"So, how's it going?" asked Peg, trying to sound as natural as she could.

"Fine." Trudy sideways-glanced her friend as they walked. "Why's your voice all weird?"

"What are you talking about? My voice is not *all weird*."

"Yes. It is. I can tell. Something's wrong," Trudy persisted.

Peg didn't speak.

"Spit it out."

"Okay... sooo," Peg began. "Clark... I mean *we*... are serious about this Key West move."

"I knew there was something." Trudy stopped in her tracks. "You have got to be kidding me. You told me you were moving to downtown Chicago. That's so unbelievably shitty."

Peg hooked her hand through Trudy's pocketed arm and nudged them forward. "Wow, I thought you gave up cursing for Lent."

"I know. I did. But since I didn't use my Sunday waiver, I can make up for it today. It's complicated but approved by the Pope. Whatever." Trudy took a deep breath and briskly faced off in front of Peg.

"I just got used to seeing the FOR SALE sign on your lawn. What about the great high-rise you saw in the city? The one with the drop-dead views of Lake Michigan and the Magnificent Mile at your doorstep? The one where you said you'd have amazing dinner parties and invite all of your suburbanite friends? You said you'd drive out here three times a week for our dog walks. You can't do that from Key West. Absolutely not. Can't you promise him more sex if he'll stop talking about Key West? Hell – promise him sex every day if you have to."

"I did that, but after all these years of marriage, that doesn't seem to work like it used to."

Peg crooked her arm around her friend's bloated winter-coat shoulders.

"I do *love* the idea of living in a high-rise in the city, but the dog's an issue. I'm having a problem finding a place that'll take a 50-pound vizsla. One apartment insisted on a picture of him, so I took the photo from across the yard thinking that maybe he'd look like the 13-pound Dachshund I entered on the application. *Now* they want to see a picture of me holding him. Maybe I shoulda said that I'm a midget. That's why the dog looked so big."

"You're not supposed to say *midget* anymore," corrected Trudy.

"Yea, I know… or even *brainstorming*. I guess that might upset people with epilepsy. Being PC's getting stressful. I love the word *brainstorming*."

"Clark is such an asshole." Trudy added, "Asshole's not a swear.

It's a body part. An unfortunate body part that has a nasty function – like Clark."

"Trudy, it's been 18 years."

Trudy stomped her boot. "*I* was the most qualified accountant interviewing for that job. Clark was personally responsible for sabotaging me. He recommended one of his brofriends. I missed out on a spectacular opportunity to work at the biggest of the Big Four accounting firms." She crossed her purple, puffy arms. "He is a big, fat, sexist, pig."

Peg waited a second then said, "He's not *that* fat." She smiled and hip-bumped Trudy. "Listen, you're great at your job and your entire company hangs on your every word. Do you think you'd have moved up so fast at a huge corporation?"

Trudy clenched her mittens. "I guess we'll never know – thanks to Clark. He's dead to me as far as I'm concerned."

"He's dead to you? Are you changing your name from Stanislowski to Corleone? What's next, a horse's head in his bed?"

Trudy stopped short. "That's really sick, Peg, how could you ever think I'd do such a thing?" She walked on. "I would put *Clark's* head in a horse's bed."

"Nice." Peg shook her big-hatted head.

"So – Clark says this. Clark says that. What does Peg have to say? Do you even know anything about Key West? Do *you* want to make a change like this?"

"Well, no... I mean yes... I mean... I don't know," Peg stammered. "With the company sold, we *can* do this, and," she ahemmed, "speaking professionally, we'll be getting the payout over ten years. It's a compromise, sure, you know Clark really pushed for the lump sum upfront, but even *he* couldn't fight the facts. The payout over ten years will be way more lucrative in the long run." Peg's boots skidded over an icy rock patch.

Trudy microphoned her mitten and belted out, "Moneymoneymoneymonneeeyy."

Peg grabbed Trudy's mitt-mike and spoke into it. "But seriously, I know I'm not going to convince you that Clark's not a bad person. But he really wants this to be a second honeymoon for us. I feel like I need to do this in support of him and our marriage."

"You're right." Trudy gazed at the ground.

"I am?" Peg looked astonished.

Trudy smirked and ran ahead. "You're *not* going to convince me that he's a good person – he's a dick." Adding over her shoulder, "Again – not a swear."

Peg jogged to catch up. "Where're the dogs?"

Trudy pointed. "Over there, on top of the hill." She turned to face the opposite direction. "Okay. Let's think about this. You don't have a job now that the company is gone. Clark will be doing consulting. What will you do there? What about friends and family?" Trudy swung around.

"You're my only family since Mom died. And you'll come to visit me. Clark'll be working from home. We'll be together. We'll do warm-weather things."

Trudy shook her head. "Do you even know how to swim?"

"I can sorta swim. I took lessons… in like the third grade." She took a breath. "It'll be good for me. Change is good." Wisely, Peg decided not to tell Trudy where she last heard that phrase.

"So, in a nutshell, your life as you know it has been traded for a palm tree."

"It's gonna be an *island* life."

"More like an *island life sentence.*"

"I know you're mad, and to make it up to you, I'll go up the disgusting hill and pick up Tucker's poop." Tucker was notorious for having the longest trail of never-ending excrement – almost always a double bagger.

Peg scrambled up the slippery incline, poop glove-bags on each hand.

Trudy yelled, "Whatever. Sure. You must honestly be thinking that you're moving to Key West if you're willing to go to such great lengths to keep me happy. I'll call you if my toilet needs plunging too."

"The house isn't sold yet." Peg used the heavy bags in each hand as ballast as she slid back to Trudy. "The market's still bad. It could take forever!"

Peg and Trudy stood side by side in front of the SOLD sign.
　　Trudy pointed at the SOLD sign and stared at Peg.
　　Trudy kicked the SOLD sign and stomped away.
　　Peg stood alone in front of the SOLD sign.

Garage Arbitrage

"Thanks for helping me with the yard sale," Peg said to Trudy. As they walked around the garage, Trudy's feet made sucky sounds in her knee-high purple polka-dot rubber boots. Her hair stuck out of a golf visor with the well-known tree on a craggy cliff logo from Pebble Beach.

"When did you go to California?" Peg pointed at Trudy's visor.

"Never been. This's my lucky garage-sale visor." Trudy took off her round glasses and cleaned them on her sweatshirt that said *Don't Trust Atoms, They Make Up Everything.*

"Sweatshirt too?" Peg grinned.

"Yup. It doubles as a dress if I need to fancy up." Trudy unscrunched the sweatshirt from around her mid-section. It draped to touch the top of her boots.

"That *is* fancy." Peg linked her friend's arm.

"I still don't see why you're moving to Key West. It's so random and unnecessary." Trudy's face reddened when she faced the front yard placard – HOUSE SOLD IN LESS THAN 30 DAYS. She unlinked her arm and shoved her hands in her gargantuan sweatshirt pockets.

Peg turned her friend away from the sign. "Yeah, we've lived in this house a long time." She avoided Trudy's glare. "But," Peg added with forced enthusiasm, "that means there's a lot of crap to sell."

"Too bad you can't sell Clark," Trudy mumbled, surveying the treasures piled up on the card tables. "You know I can't be mad during a garage sale, my Achilles heel. Last year, I got a video camera for twenty-five cents at an estate sale. I had to haggle with the widow. Tough old bird."

"You haggled with a woman… for her dead husband's video camera… for a quarter?" Peg's eyes grew wide.

"Yes. But it didn't come with a charger cord. That's proved to be a problem."

Peg half-listened to her friend and scanned the drab, wet skies. She rubbed the arms of her down coat. "I hope the weather holds."

"A little freezing, slushy rain won't hold back the diehard yard-salers." No sooner had the prophecy been spoken than the junk junkies started to circle the cul-de-sac.

The first customer gravitated toward the holiday table, and picked up one of the kitchen towels. The towel was embroidered with a Christmas tree and the saying *I love you this and every other Christmas.* Peg remembered when Clark had given her that towel. He'd wrapped it around a bottle of wine and placed it in a silver and gold basket with two green crystal wine glasses. The snow-storm had prohibited the usual family and friend festivities. The room had been cozy, Christmas music had played, the tree lights had twinkled and –

The towel... I love that towel.

Overcome with emotion, Peg lurched over the table and grabbed the towel from the unsuspecting shopper's hand.

Trudy hustled over to diffuse the situation. Waving three other colorful towels in the customer's direction, she blurted, "These towels are a better deal – three for the price of one."

The woman initially resisted, until she saw Peg wipe her eyes and blow her nose on the Christmas towel. Making a face, the shopper snatched the three-pack from Trudy and tossed the towels in her plastic grocery bag.

Meanwhile, Peg scanned the garage.

In the corner, a grandmotherly looking woman inspected the glassware. She lifted *the* pair of green crystal wine glasses and held them up to the lamplight. Green reflections of cut glass discoed across the ceiling.

The glasses... I love those green wine glasses. CLARK said they match my eyes.

Satisfied with their condition, the grandmother delicately placed the crystal glasses in a silver and gold basket.

The basket... I love that basket.

It was too much. Peg made her move, but not fast enough. The elderly customer saw Peg coming.

Assuming a sumo wrestler stance, Grandma was ready for a match.

Peg bobbed.

Grams weaved.

Peg lunged.

Grams lurched.

"What are you doing?" Trudy grabbed Peg from behind, her hands hooked around Peg's waist.

"I can't let these go." Peg had a grip of one side of the basket handle. The resolute Grams matched her grip on the other side.

The tug of war continued. Peg's neck veins bulged. "This is my life here on display. For cents on the dollar."

"This was your idea!" Trudy said through clenched jaw.

"I can't do it," Peg wailed as the basket handle snapped in half.

The two glasses twirled into the air. Peg caught the stem of one glass at the same moment the other one shattered on the ground. Peg fell backward on top of Trudy.

Other than a slight two-step and grimace, the old lady was unmoved both physically and emotionally. She shook her head in disgust, mouthing curse words as she walked down the driveway. Other shoppers in the garage chucked their possible purchases onto the closest table and followed suit.

The two friends untangled their limbs on the cold cement floor. Tears flowed from Peg's face as she cradled the goblet in the towel.

Trudy brushed the green glass shards from her butt. "This is going to be a *very* long day."

Moving Out

The team of suburban Chicago college boys from A+ Moving Company were fast and efficient. Their matching tee shirts, khakis, and polite enthusiasm gave them a boy scout quality. The foreman shouted echoey instructions up the hallway, while the men strapped impossible amounts of weight to their backs. They responded to the boss with effortless, cheery affirmatives. In less than four hours, the house was reduced to carpet imprints and nail holes. Peg wandered the rooms attempting to fluff the rugs with the toe of her shoe, but the holes were there to stay.

The foreman closed the back of the moving truck with a loud clang and then climbed into the cab of the giant semi. He smiled and waved as the truck chugged away. Peg waved back limp-wristed and watched 20 years roll out of the neighborhood.

Peg noticed Trudy coming up the driveway while Clark made room for Nipper in the car's back seat, amidst lampshades and plants. The dog sat at attention. Unblinking, he willed the humans into the car. Peg's legs felt weak.

"You are such a bitch." Trudy's lip quivered.

"I know I am." Peg's voice cracked.

And then the dam broke. They sobbed in each other's arms until Peg pulled herself free and jammed herself into the passenger seat. As the car backed away from the curb, she could hear Trudy crying out through tears and cupped hands, "Clark, you're an asshole. You suck."

Clark rolled up the car windows.

They turned right at the corner past big-boobed Barb's house and then right again toward signs for Route 355 South.

Peg cried. She wept. She bawled. Nipper licked her ear. Clark glanced at her sideways. "Adventure time," he said with a big smile. "It will all be fine."

Peg lifted her head from her hands, blew her nose and mustered up a non-gasping breath. "I know," she lied.

The Drive

Nipper settled easily into the 26-hour journey. He enjoyed the cave-like enclosure of the back seat, the humming of the engine and the proximity of his humans. When the car stopped, he would perform the obligatory squirt on rest-stop garbage cans, happy to take in the exotic scents of all who went before him.

First hour of the drive:

Clark: "What d'you want to listen to?"

Peg (massaging Clark's neck with her left hand): "I don't care, whatever you want."

Clark: "I'm turning on the air conditioning. I don't think I'll need the heated steering wheel anymore."

Peg: "Look, the trees are blooming already down here. It'll be nice to see flowers earlier in the year."

Clark: "There are flowers year round in Key West, not to mention sunshine. I'm so sick of gray and gloomy."

Peg: "I'll like that and Nipper does love to sunbathe. He'll be happy too."

Clark: "Happy dog, happy life."

Peg: "I have to pee."

Clark: "Sure. We'll stop at the next exit."

Peg: "I love you and my bladder loves you."

The fourteenth hour of the drive:

Clark: "I'd like to drive all the way through today."

Peg: "What? That's another 14 hours. We did 12 yesterday."

Clark: "I'm not staying at another fleabag doggie hotel. It cost a fortune and was a dump. I'm on a roll and wanta get there."

Peg: "My butt hurts already and it's only been a couple of hours."

Clark: "And don't drink any liquids 'cause I'm not stopping."

Peg: "My bladder has changed its mind about you."

The twentieth hour of the drive:

Peg: "Why are we listening to Spanish music?"

Clark: "It's not Spanish, it's Cuban music."

Peg: "Oh."

(Pause)

Peg: "Why are we listening to Cuban music?"

Clark: "We're going to be living 90 miles from Havana. We need to start acclimating."

Peg: "Listen, Ricky Ricardo, it's been eight solid hours of salsa. Can we please listen to a song in English?"

Clark: "It's not salsa, it's rhumba."

Peg: "Okay then – listen, Ricky... um... Martin, turn it off. We're in Florida and I can get a gun at the nearest grocery store. I'm not afraid to use it."

Clark: "Fine."

(Silence)

Clark: "Ricky Martin is Puerto Rican – just so you know."

Peg: "Stop at the Minimart right now."

Passing Miami after 23 hours in the car, Clark opened the window to let in the sea air. Nipper's ears and lips flapped behind the driver's seat. When the car approached the first bridge, Peg felt her lungs and stomach combine to make a new body organ.

Google says there are 42 bridges. Okay... breathe... sing.

"When the red, red robin comes bob, bob, bobbin' along. Like a bridge over troubled–"

No, stop. Bad song.

"This little light of mine. I'm gonna let it shine."

Clark remarked, "Singing seems to be working."

"Kind of. But I'm not driving and these have been *short* bridges." Peg flapped her hands to increase blood flow.

"Okay, listen, we're halfway down the Keys. Let's stop in

Islamorada for a dog and–," Clark exaggerated a head swirl to look at Peg, "mental health break."

"Good idea. I need a walk to reset my central nervous system." Peg wiped her clammy fingers on her shirt.

They pulled off Route 1 and into a large open park area. Peg got out of the car, placed her hands on her hips and arched her achy back. "Ahhh. Freedom. Feels good to be out of the car. C'mon, Nipper." She opened up the back door and the dog bounced to the pavement.

"I just have to check some messages. Gonna make sure the moving company didn't reach out with any problems." Clark stood next to the car with his phone in his hand.

"We'll be walking over there." Peg saw that Clark was already plugged in to his phone. "Okay?" No response. "I hope we don't get eaten by zombies."

"That sounds good," Clark muttered.

"All right then. Let's go, Nipper, and watch out for zombies 'cause we're on our own apparently." The dog beelined up the concrete steps to a large monument in the middle of the square. Dragging Peg behind him, he stopped short of a plaque and lifted his leg.

"Nipper, no. This is history you're peeing on."

Peg read the historical marker:

"DEDICATED TO THE MEMORY OF THE CIVILIANS AND WAR VETERANS WHOSE LIVES WERE LOST IN THE HURRICANE OF SEPTEMBER SECOND 1935."

Nipper stopped mid-squirt, then continued on full stream ahead when he realized that Peg wasn't paying attention.

Hurricane. So awful. Hundreds of deaths. No escape.

Peg glanced away from her reading and saw the yellow puddle at her feet. "C'mon, Nipper, let's go before we get arrested for defacing public property." The dog trotted next to her as she yelled-slash-jogged back to the car. "The entire railroad system was destroyed. The whole thing."

"What?" Clark looked up from his phone.

"The hurricane took out everything and *everyone*. There are pictures. It's horrific." Peg pointed to the placard by the monument that now had a distinctive yellow line running down the middle of it.

Clark shook his head. "That was a long time ago – before early-warning systems and advanced technology." He got into the driver's seat and started the car engine.

Peg opened the door for Nipper and he snuggled into his back-seat burrow. "I'm sorry, but being on a bridge is scary enough, but driving on one during a hurricane? It's–" She shut her car door.

Clark interrupted her, "–not going to happen. You'll be fine." The back tires spun in the gravel as they merged back onto Route 1.

Peg averted her eyes as they passed the rusty cadaverous remnants of the old Flagler railroad looming out of the ocean. Its lifeless form a constant reminder of the brute force and unpredictability of Mother Nature.

Stop imagining people careening off the structure and being swallowed up by the raging waters. Helpless. Screaming.

Her newly formed lung-slash-stomach welcomed the intestines to the party.

Then – IT appeared.

Out of the clear blue skies, there IT was.

The SEVEN-MILE BRIDGE.

Strung out like a lounging snake, IT bided ITS time, waiting to take ITS prey.

"I think I'm going to faint. I really can't breathe," she wheezed.

"I can't stop here." The oncoming traffic whizzed past. "Try singing again."

"Passing out… not kidding."

"Do you think it's safe for me to be distracted, worrying about you, while driving on a bridge that you are afraid for me to drive across?"

Even in her oxygen-depleted state, she had to admit that he *did* have a point.

"Supercalifragilisticexpialidocious. Even though the sound of it is something quite atrocious," Peg squeaked.

Clark's neck vein receded and a tiny smile formed. "If you say it loud enough you'll always sound precocious."

Peg focused her stare at her husband's profile, and her voice gained strength. "Supercalifragilisticexpialidocious."

Laughing in unison, they launched into, "Um–dittle–ittl–um–dittle–I, Um–dittle–ittl–um–dittle–I…"

And so they sang until the song ended and the bridge connected with the earth. She had made it – as a passenger – across a BIG bridge.

"See? You were fine."

"I know."

But she wasn't.

Meeting the Neighbors

"Hallooo." Peg's voice echoed through the empty house.

All of Peg's secret wishes for a botched closing so they could move back to Chicago were dashed.

The money wired.

The realtors took their envelopes.

The title company took their envelope.

Peg and Clark Savage took the keys to their island home.

"The sellers said the cleaners should be here. I'll take Nipper on a run before the storm hits." Clark tied his Nikes and put his baseball cap on backward.

"It might be nice if you could–" Peg heard the door slam. "Whatever… or perhaps not."

Peg wandered around the corner of the front hallway toward the stairs. She jumped with a start when a small, round black woman stood in front of her – out of nowhere. She wore a vibrant colored headscarf and beads on her wrists and ankles. Her feet were flat and bare.

"Oh. Hi. Sorry. You scared me. I'm Peg… new owner. Nice to meet you." She held out her hand.

The woman held out a wrinkled hand and seized Peg's. Placing her other weather-worn hand over the handshake, the woman firmly pressed the hand sandwich to her large, sagging breasts. "I am Jacinta." Her lips drained of color as she gummed a broad grin.

Thinking that it might be a custom, Peg held her hand to Jacinta's bosoms for what seemed to be a very long time. She returned the smile. "Yes, well, good. Okay. I'm… well… we're just here… I mean my husband and my dog… they're… uh… coming soon… and the movers."

Jacinta released Peg's hand and opened the front door of the house. She stood on the wooden porch and stared at the ceiling painted a brilliant azure. She motioned for Peg to follow. Waving her short arms theatrically in a rainbow shape, she pointed upward with a bony finger. "Dis good dis blue. Keep dis. Haints can't get to you. Dey don't like water. Haints can't cross water. Blue keep dem away." She closed her eyes, as if in prayer.

Peg broke the silence. "Um, excuse me. What's a haint? I'm from Chicago. It snows a lot up there and I don't think we have haints... probably too cold... it can get foggy too..."

"Ghos. Evil spirits," Jacinta groaned, breaking her trance. "This old house. Many die who came here. Many want to come back. Blue keep dem away." She flapped her arms like a bird and then padded back into the house.

Peg stood motionless, staring at the porch ceiling. Her mouth dropped open when she noticed sections where the paint had worn off. A large gust of wind blew the ever-present island coral dust in a whirlpool along the edge of the decking. She felt a chill. "Um, excuse me again, like, um, how many died, do you think? Why do they want to come back?" Hair standing on end, Peg searched the house, but Jacinta was gone. Out of the side window, a three-wheeled motor scooter hauling a wagon of cleaning supplies zoomed by.

Peg was by herself in the house.

She hoped.

Moving In

The wind slammed the door backward against the wall as Clark and Nipper entered the house. What was once a sunny day, suddenly turned dark. Peg startled and clutched her chest.

"What's the matter? You look like you saw a ghost." Clark fingered the doorknob indent that was a permanent fixture on the wall.

"A *haint*." Peg rushed over to close the door. "The cleaning lady creeped me out. She told me they have ghosts here. Lots of them – undead called *haints*."

Clark rolled his eyes.

"Did you know that, right this very minute, hundreds, maybe thousands of undead who have been in this house are clammering to get back in? I bet 'haint alert' was not included in the home inspection. Apparently the blue porch ceiling is *all* that protects us from our souls being sucked out, doomed to roam forever in limbo."

"So, we are protected then. Then there h'aint no problem. Nyuck, nyuck, nyuck." Clark snapped his fingers while skipping backward in a Three Stooges move.

Oh, how she hated it when he looked so cute.

Peg willed herself back to her worries. "No. Actually there *are* chunks of blue paint missing from the front porch. I mean, how many undead can fit through? Personally, I would prefer zero."

Not helping her cause any, a crash of thunder shook the house. The black skies relieved themselves of their heavy load. The noise was deafening against the metal roof.

"Oh my God," she yelled. "Look at the water. I've never seen anything like it... like it's being poured out of a... Oh, I think I see a moving truck out there." She yanked at the door, but the bloated wood refused to budge. "I just shut this door.

And now I can't open it." She pulled again using all of her strength.

Clark came to her rescue. The door succumbed reticently – first the top half, then the bottom half – making a *boing* sound as it released its sticky grip. "This is the rainy season. Storms don't last long, only brief shower bursts."

Peg strained to see through the waterfall.

A *small* yellow moving truck bearing the name High End Moving parked in front of the house. All of their belongings had been packed in a *big* yellow moving truck in Illinois. Peg didn't recognize the driver either.

"Hi. You must have the wrong house. This is not our truck," she screamed from the door, trying not to get wet.

"Yes, ma'am, it is. We hadta unload the big truck into two smaller trucks 'cause the streets is too small. We'll go back and git the other truck later."

"What?" The roof raindrop noise was getting louder.

"Some stuff got a lil wet when we took it outta the semi," the large man said as he approached the door. "I'm Big Jim by the way. They call me BJ." He most definitely was BIG Jim – a full 6-foot-5 both tall and wide. His head was the size of a prize pumpkin with a row of large straight teeth showing under a gargantuan Yosemite Sam mustache. A limp, wet cigarette hung out of his mouth over a skull and crossbones tattoo that extended from the bottom of his chin to his large Adam's apple. When he spoke, the crossbones rubbed together like sticks igniting a fire.

Two co-workers, shirtless and soaked, emerged from the cab of the truck. Peg was sure that the one with the gold tooth had bullet-hole scars on his chest – just above his pierced nipples. The other one was bearded with dreadlocks and a tattoo across his chest that said, *If you can read this the bitch fell off.* Both had serious butt-crack exposure.

"O-kaay." Peg grabbed Clark's arm and spoke in low tones. "Well, Bee Jaay, who looks like Blackbeard, is here with two other guys from *America's Most Wanted* to unload half of our soggy belongings. God knows where the other half is. Probably being bootlegged on the black market. Where are the clean-cut men with logo tee shirts that loaded our stuff in Illinois?"

Peg peeked out of the door through diminishing raindrops to see Nipper up on his hind legs, hugging Big Jim. The man returned the nuzzle, cooing baby talk in the dog's ear.

So much for the guard dog.

Clark grabbed an umbrella and walked into the drizzle to shake the driver's gigantic hand. Peg wondered if she had packed hand sanitizer in her travel bag.

The assorted furniture and piles of water-stained boxes made their way out of the first truck, and, just when the house refused to take on any more, the second truck showed up. Peg wedged her way around the melee, trying not to run into any of the movers, who reeked of smoldering Roquefort.

When the men lounged on the front porch to smoke, she felt sure that if there were such things as haints, they would look exactly like this group of beings. Their loud voices carried into the hallway, telling of their plan for a big night out on the town in Key West. Peg imagined these pirates walking around her small Midwestern town. The shop owners on Main Street would likely call the authorities to report these suspicious characters who were most certainly not going to buy a scented candle or paisley overnight bag.

I could use a scented candle right now.

The pungent marijuana smell from her college years wafted through the crack in the front door. She wrinkled her nose as Clark entered the house.

"What the...?" She pushed Clark into the bathroom and shut the door.

In hushed tones Peg said, "Did you see those reprobates on our front stoop? What will the neighbors think? What are we going to do about it?"

Two tendrils of sweet-smelling smoke trickled out of Clark's nostrils.

"Really? You're kidding. What's next? Heroin on the back patio?" Peg coughed and waved away the stinky air. "It's against the law, by the way."

She opened the bathroom door and face-planted directly into Big Jim's animated skull and crossbones Adam's apple. His unibrow raised in amused curiosity when he witnessed Peg *then* Clark exit the room.

"No. It's not what you think. We were looking at something... together... in here." She pointed to the toilet, shook her head, pointed at the shower then, rethinking that movement, motioned to the sink faucet.

"Yes, ma'am. We're done. Y'all have a good evening." BJ sniggered as he left.

Peg could hear the group's raucous laughter as they climbed into the truck.

"I wonder what he thinks we were doing in there?"

Clark grabbed his wife by the waist. "Gettin' a bad reputation already." He winked. "But a *bad* reputation is a *good* reputation in Key West."

"Perfect. We'll be the topic of all the trash talk tonight."

"Hey, we'll be popular. People will be lined up for a reefer and a bathroom quickie."

Seeing he was enjoying this topic, Peg ignored the comment, not wanting to further the conversation.

"Why don't *we* go out and have a night on the town? Celebrate." Clark's eyes were bloodshot.

Peg surveyed the mountains of boxes. "I don't even know where the sheets are to make the bed. I'd like to find the towels too." Before Clark could object she added, "You go ahead. It's not like you'll be that much help right now in your current condition. Nipper and I will stay here."

Clark kissed her nose. "I'll be back soon." He grabbed his phone off of a pile of boxes and left.

Nipper found a corner to lie down. "Let's get started." She sat on the floor next to him. Rubbing her temples, she sighed.

Where am I going to put all of this?

Trudy was right – shoulda let that lady have the Christmas towel.

Morning in Paradise

"These past couple of weeks have been kinda like a dream to me." Peg ruffled Clark's hair on the way to the cupboard for a coffee cup. "It's all so new – like a beautiful strange planet. Maybe not quite as hot as Mars, but close."

Clark typed at his computer, "Uh huh."

Peg poured herself a cup of coffee. "The sunset was amazing last night. I didn't realize it's the clouds that make it spectacular."

"Mmmm. Right."

"And the fish taco at the pier? Absolutely delicious, best I've ever tasted – so fresh and flaky. I'd go back there every night." She blew on the steam rising from her cup.

Clark looked up from the screen, "I have to go to Cuba."

"Cuba? Why?" Peg choked on her sip of coffee.

"A company has asked me to consult for a start-up. Things are opening up with the US."

"Cuba?"

"I know. It's an amazing opportunity."

Peg made a face.

Clark was undeterred. "We discussed that I'd be doing some consulting."

"I didn't think you'd have to start working so soon. And, I thought your work would be from the house, not from Cuba." The caffeine and humidity produced tiny water beads on her upper lip.

"This company needs my help setting up their communications. We Americans take cell phones and the Internet for granted, but Cubans have very limited accessibility. Gonna be groundbreaking work – helping millions of underprivileged people. This is a chance for me to do something on a global level. I need to go there to assess the resources already in place."

"Tough to argue when you use words like Americans and *underprivileged* and *global*." Peg wrinkled her brow. "It seems so soon for you to leave, when we just got here." She plopped her elbows on the counter and cupped her cheeks in her hands. "You don't even speak Spanish. Are you the right person to set up communications when you can't communicate?"

"I've been working with a translator. She's been instrumental in organizing the work." Clark avoided Peg's eyes. He stood up and talked over his shoulder as he walked into the bedroom. "Listen, it's only 90 miles away – closer than the nearest Target."

"How long will you be gone?" Peg shouted, not realizing he had come back into the room.

Clark grimaced at her yelling. "No more than a week or so – be back before you know it." He patted her on the back. "Hey, where's my swimsuit?"

Peg wished she could be happier about his selfless charity.

"Hello? Swimsuit?" Clark interrupted her thoughts.

"Oh... uh... swimsuit? I think it's in the closet with the towels and hacksaw. No not that one, that's the coat and dog food closet."

"Ah, that makes perfect sense." Clark nodded his head in an exaggerated up and down motion.

Peg jumped back as a bright green gecko slithered down the inside of the closet door. "Yick, I'll never get used to those things... creepy and crawly." She pranced in a circle, waving her hands.

"They're three inches long. What're they going to do to you?"

Nipper took notice and began a slow army crawl toward the creature, counting on the element of surprise.

"Heart attack... they give me the willies."

"Hey, we don't need these coats anymore. You'd have extra space if you got rid of them." Clark tossed the heavy outerwear onto the floor on top of the already growing pile of former closet occupants as he continued his search.

"It *is* possible that I'll go to back to Chicago sometime, you know." Peg swallowed the tiny lump in her throat.

"Ah ha. Here it is." He tugged out a bright floral suit from under a pile of towels. The towel tower tumbled off the shelf. "Right, of course, but not in the winter. How could you leave this?" Clark pointed to the blue sky and green palm fronds showing through the picture window.

"It *is* beautiful," she admitted, then glanced down at the floor. She squatted to pick up the pen that had fallen out of a coat pocket. Holding it up, she inspected the side. "The company logo... I remember when I had these made." She gathered the towels to stack them back where they belonged.

"I leave on Friday at eleven in the morning. Direct from Key West, 35-minute flight."

"Friday? Like... this Friday? Two days from now Friday?" Peg ceased folding straight-edge creases in a towel on the floor.

"Peg, it's not a big deal. I'll be gone a week."

"I thought you'd be working from home for any consulting once we moved here."

"They want to know the on-site feasibility of the project. Needs to be decided as soon as possible."

Peg brightened. "Why don't I come too? I am the financial expert. I could make sure the project stays on budget."

"No budget yet. No real company. It's just a consult."

Peg lowered her eyelids.

He leaned down and lifted her chin. "Nipper will keep you company and I'll be back in a week."

Hearing his name, the dog looked over at them, allowing the trapped lizard a welcome escape.

Lucky lizard.

Peg watched as Clark stripped naked in the middle of the kitchen and put on his swimsuit.

How can men do that? They don't even care who sees them? Wow, he does have a great butt.

"Here, take the new beach towel. It's bigger." She tossed it across the floor in Clark's direction.

Clark's eyes met Peg's. He sucked in his stomach while patting the middle-aged layers. "I'm working on getting rid of this. Wanna go for a swim in the ocean with me?" He grabbed his goggles out of the beach bag.

"Okay," she said, forcing her brain to stop calculating how

many hours until 11am on Friday. "I'll get the leash and bring Nipper too."

"How great is this that we can walk to the ocean for a swim?" Clark exuded happiness.

"So great," Peg replied with fabricated eagerness. "Come on, Nipper, let's go."

"Aren't you going to wear your suit?" Clark slathered on the sunscreen. "It's the *beach*."

"Right, I guess so."

The leashed dog followed Peg around the room as she located her new suit hanging next to the yard rake in the vacuum-cleaner closet. Nipper nudged his nose into the door to enter the bathroom with her. "Sorry, Nip. Not enough room for both of us in here." Peg shut the door. The dog plopped down with a loud thud.

Not wanting even the mirror to see her naked, she moved away from its judging eye. She shimmied the triple-ruched, ultra-slimming suit up her thighs with exaggerated hip swirls, but the stubborn one-piece bunched at her waist and refused to go any higher.

What is happening? This fit when I tried it on in the store.

Her sticky skin fought the spandex. She attempted to find the top part of the suit.

Is this suit made of double-sided tape? Is it on backward?

Seeing what looked like a strap, she hunkered down and yanked it up over her right arm. One breast encased in a swimsuit knot and the other dangling homeless, Peg forced herself upright, only to produce the most perfect and fantastic of wedgies. Sweat trickled...

"What are you doing in there?" Clark called out from the back door. "I'm ready to go."

"Go ahead. I'll meet you there." Peg tried not to sound out of breath.

"You bring the dog so I can start to swim."

"Fine. Just go." The bathroom walls closed in on her as she realized she had pulled the left strap over the right arm. No matter how hard she heaved, yanked or contorted, the spider web of a bathing suit held fast.

I think I'm going to have to cut this thing off. No you are NOT. That is a one-hundred-dollar Nordstrom bathing suit. You are NOT going to cut it off.

The dog barked in concern when he heard the scuffle coming from inside the bathroom.

"I'm coming, Nipper. Don't worry. No need for both of us to be worried."

Deep breath. You can do this.

In order to remove the possibility of a vertical bisection, she morphed her body into a Quasimodo shape, and wrangled the tenacious suit back down to the inner tube of five minutes ago. Composing herself, she unraveled the rubbery roll until the straps became visible and she could stretch the bra cups over the proper inhabitants. Snap. Success.

Feeling triumphant, she looked into the mirror.

Rashy, pasty, hairy in the wrong places.

And she had to pee.

The Sand is Always Whiter...

Peg paused to observe the vibrant purples and reds of the bougainvillea as she made her way to the beach. The outlines of the palm trees along the blue horizon formed postcard splendor. The water in the Gulf of Mexico had so many variations of color it reminded her of a chart on a paint wheel: shades like Mermaid Net, Salty Tear and Phantom Mist.

In stark contrast, the white sidewalk blended with the white road in the whiteness of the sunlight. The polarized sunglasses couldn't prevent spots from forming in her vision. The laser beam rays of sun prickled her skin.

And summer doesn't officially start until next week.

Peg's new full-length cover-up clung to her inner thighs as the moisture built up. Tugging the dress away from her body as she moved, she wondered if the sausage-casing bathing suit would sizzle into her, forming a permanent second skin.

Note to self – no more wearing long melty polyester dresses – no matter how cute.

To top it off, the giant black hat that looked so stylish in the store trapped heat like an incinerator.

Nipper walked on high alert while stalking roosters and chickens and baby chicks and pigeons and egrets and herons – bird-dog sensory overload. After a couple of blocks, the heat of the day overpowered instinct. Nipper gave up the quest, tongue panting and drooping.

They stopped in front of the White Street Pier sign. She saw Clark's towel on the beach next to the stairway entrance to the water. Two homeless men plugged in their smart phones in the outlets on the electric poles.

Hmm – high-tech homeless – maybe I should ask them how to connect my printer to Wi-Fi.

One of the men called out to her, "Hey, beautiful. You're HOT."

You have no idea.

She blushed through her hotness and quickened her step.

Nipper pulled the leash, searching for shady spots. He stopped in his tracks when the tiniest white and brown chihuahua in a pink, fluffy tutu strutted by. The minuscule dog barked and growled. Nipper stood statue-still, unable to understand why a rodent would be wearing sequins.

"Lulu. You leave that poor big dog alone. Pick on someone your own size." The owner of the chihuahua giggled and scooped her up. Lulu snarled while attempting to bite him. "You little beast," the man said in a sing-song voice and tossed her in a purple beaded shoulder pouch with rainbow fringe, crusted with gems – a blend of Dolce & Gabbana, Louis Vuitton and Chanel, but for dogs.

"Sorry. She only acts like this when she likes you," the man said. He zipped up the dog in the satchel and picked up his bicycle from the ground. As the two of them rode away, the sound of squeaky wheels and muffled yipping faded into the distance.

"I can't imagine what she'd be like if she *didn't* like you," Peg said as she leaned down to pet Nipper's hot head.

"Come on in," Clark yelled from waist-high turquoise water. "What took you so long?" He splashed and rolled on his back. Peg could just make out his silhouette in the glistening water. A barrier of seaweed undulated with the tides in-between the shore's edge and the frolicking swimmer.

"The stairs look slippery." Peg pointed to the green, algae-covered steps – swimming anxiety kicking in.

"Look. It's shallow all the way to the end of the pier. Jump in." He porpoise-dove under the water, coming up 15 feet from the shore.

Peg pulled off her sweaty cover-up and spread it out to dry on the pebbly sand. As she tugged the suit down over the problem areas in the front and back and sides, she thought she saw a couple next to her shade their eyes from the glare of sun off of her translucent skin.

What? Have you never seen Chicago skin before?

The dog sat on the sand, panting as Peg surveyed the situation. Beyond the stairs, slimy, seaweedy things floated in clumpy masses. She could see fish darting in and out.

She pinched her nose to close out the hot-summer-day-garbage-truck smell wafting up from the water.

Clark laughed. "It's low tide. That's why there's so much seaweed. It's beautiful out here once you get past it." He spat a fountain of salt water into the air.

That might be, but it didn't necessarily make her feel any better about the stink. She put one foot down on the top step, slipped a couple of inches and cringed as the sludge enveloped her toes. With a high-pitched screech she jumped over the steps directly into the sea grass. The bottom was rocky and shallow, forcing her to either stand on the sharp-edged coral or dog paddle through the weeds. Lifting her feet and thrashing her arms she attempted to carve her way. The long brown pods tangled in her curly hair and wrapped around her neck and armpits. Constricting tighter and tighter, they pulled her down. Gasping for breath, she stood up in the hip-deep water. A shawl of muck and weeds outfitted her in the most impressive swamp-monster fashion. Her feet instinctively set course for the stairway, sacrificing their soles along the way.

The stairs were unclimbable in their sliminess. She was forced to go up backward – hands, butt, feet, hands, butt, feet – scraping and amassing goo along the way. The previously unmovable swimsuit slid easily in its new greasy coating, forming an impressive mass of material between her newly exposed blotchy, muddy buttocks.

Nipper waited for her, alternately chewing on his footpad and pacing back and forth. Once Peg made it to the top, Nipper licked the green grime off of her back while she released the stranglehold of sea-tangle from her shoulders, neck and face. Realizing that she had forgotten a towel, she wiped off the guck with her hands.

Avoiding the steps, Clark hopped up the sea wall, using his upper body strength in a gymnastics move. "You'll get the hang of it. The water's warm. Not like Lake Michigan, is it?" He wiped his face with his towel.

Peg plucked the sea grass out of her hair with grubby, stained fingers.

Nope. It's not like Lake Michigan.

Together by Herself

Sprawled diagonally across the bed, Peg watched the ceiling fan whirl off-kilter. The long stem of the fan wobbled.

This doesn't look safe. If it falls, it will kill me. Who would know? No one will miss me for days.

On the chair next to the bed, Nipper watched her watch the fan. "Why should we get up?" She lifted her knees and shoved her feet back under the sheets. "This is luxury, lounging in bed. No early-morning walk to jam in before the job. No alarm. No reason to make a pot of coffee – just for me. Unless you would like some? No, don't get started, it's an addiction." The dog cocked his head sideways as she spoke.

"I wonder how they are doing at the old office. I gave them my number in case they had any questions. Maybe I should call them to check in." She lifted the blanket and sat up. Anticipating some action, Nipper sat up too. "No, they would have called if they needed help. It went fine during the transition." She plopped back down on the bed. The dog slumped over his paws. Peg looked at the clock.

Nine thirty here… so eight thirty in Chicago. Trudy'll be back from their walk before work.

She reached for the computer.

"He's gone where?" The computer screen showed the empty chair, where Trudy's face should have been.

"Cuba. But only for a week or so." Peg analyzed the video image of herself that split the screen. She took the rubber band from her wrist and pulled her frizzy hair back in a ponytail. Changing her mind, she shook her hair out of the band and fluffed it with her fingers. Not satisfied, she gathered it into a bun on the top of her head. *Ugh.* She hit the key to disable her videoconferencing camera. *Problem solved.* "Can you hear me? What are you doing?"

"I'm putting my socks on." Trudy's head popped up and her face appeared on the screen. "Why can't I see *you?*"

"I turned off my camera. It's for your own good."

"Yes. I have very high fashion standards, as you know." Trudy pushed her nose up in the air with her pointer finger and crossed her eyes. "What a wad. He's left you by yourself already? What about *I'll work from home. We'll be together?* BS. What is he doing in Cuba? Fraternizing with Fidel?"

"Fidel is dead, Trudy."

"Whatever."

"He's consulting for a start-up. I'm sure that this is a one-time thing. It's only for a week or so."

"He moved you there and now you're alone. Jesus, I've had bad perms that lasted longer than that."

"It's okay. I have stuff to do."

"Like what? Walk the dog. Then what? Thanks to Clark, you don't have a job anymore, remember? You've unpacked that tiny house. You don't have any friends there… Are you still in *bed?*"

Peg checked to make sure the camera icon on the screen was still crossed off. She hustled out of bed.

"No!"

"Well, what *are* you going to do?"

"Catch up on reading."

"Then what?"

"Clean the house. Do yard work."

"Every day?"

"Walk the dog again… I don't know. I'm figuring it out."

"It seems to me you shoulda done that before you moved." Trudy paused. Her voice quieted. "I miss you and Nipper. I cry every day when we drive past your house. I'm never going to get over this."

"I miss you and Tucker too." Peg's eyes watered.

"Okay. I gotta go to work. Let's talk later." Trudy looked away from the camera.

"Okay. Bye."

Trudy disconnected the signal. Peg looked at the frozen screen-shot of Trudy's profile.

"Not the same as playing with them in person, is it?"

Nipper agreed.

Email from Clark to Peg

```
Hi. I've tried to call, but there is
absolutely no cell phone reception for
international calls. The Internet is a joke
too. They need so much help getting this set
up. Right now I'm standing on a street corner
with hundreds of other people trying to get
a signal. I've attached a picture of where
I am. Check it out. It's crazy. It's like
New Year's Eve at Times Square. The people
here are very nice and ready to learn but I
underestimated how much work it will be to
set this up. It's like caveman times. Looks
like I'll have to stay here for at least a
couple of weeks, maybe more. I hope you get
this. I've been dropped three times already.
I'll try to email again as soon as I can.
Email me back with news. Love you and Nip-
per.
```

Peg opened the attachment with a picture of Clark in a crowd of dark-skinned, young Cubans huddled in masses around their phones. He had a "see, I told you" smile on his face with his palms held up, as if the crowd was on display. She clicked off the computer screen and began to pace the room.

Two weeks? Maybe longer? No communication? Oh, stop being such a wimp. Do you think anyone will feel sorry for you in your house in

Key West? I know, but this doesn't feel like a second honeymoon by myself. Stop.

Peg picked up the calendar propped up on the desk. Above the month of June there was a picture of a smiling man stranded on an island, drinking out of a coconut. The message under the photo read, "Life is 10% of what happens to you and 90% of how you react to it."

Right, smile now, Mr. Man. Do you know that coconuts can kill you in a storm? I'm 100% sure you're not gonna react too well to an 80-mile-per-hour coconut to the head.

She happy-faced the day on the calendar when Clark would return and looked past the condensation on the kitchen windows.

Getting dark. More rain soon.

Her phone buzzed. Her heart leapt. She swiped the device. "Do you want to consolidate your credit?"

Ugh.

Peg tossed her cell phone onto the couch. "I guess I don't need to carry this around with me."

Nipper lifted his head at the possibility of something being thrown for him.

"Okay, let's go for a walk."

Saturday: Peg and Nipper stood next to the sticky door waiting for the rain to stop.

Sunday: Peg and Nipper sat next to the swollen door waiting for the rain to stop.

Monday, Tuesday, Wednesday, Thursday, Friday: Peg and Nipper lay on the floor next to the stuck door waiting for the rain to stop.

Saturday Again

On the first clear morning of this rainiest of rainy seasons, Peg boinged open the sodden door.

Nipper twirled out of the house. They danced around the deck with new-found enthusiasm and cheerfulness. Even though her sunglasses remained stubbornly fogged, she saw the day in a new light – sunlight. "I think we're gonna be okay." She took in a deep belly breath and the dog wagged his tail.

Hands on hips, she observed the stacks of leaves and giant palm fronds strewn about. "Not enough to do? Hah, this yard looks like a war zone." The dog sniffed around, concentrating his efforts on the back corner of the fence. "My God, look at the size of these. Glad we were not under there when they fell. They're huge." Peg chatted with the dog as she dragged one of the 14-foot fronds out of the gate. She warily observed the coconut trees across the street, swaying innocuously in the breeze.

She waved hello to the sweaty workman in the neighbor's yard. The bandana around his head worked with dam-like precision to keep moisture out of his eyes. Shovel in hand, his muscles bulged as he dug a hole in the crusty coral earth. Short and stocky, he looked like the kind of guy who could wrestle an alligator and win. He moved with purpose, but took the time to say "ehlow" back to Peg.

His helper pushed a wheelbarrow with a medium-sized flowery shrub tipping precariously to one side, the root ball unraveling as it bumped about.

"Bee carefool wiz zat," the do-ragged boss said to the pusher. The rail-thin, shirtless man nodded his head then stood silently next to the hole, waiting further instructions. His vacant stare had the look of the possible "undead" that were most likely wandering around the island.

Peg gathered the behemoth palms one at a time and hauled them out into the street.

"Nipper, what are you doing over there?"

The dog refused to be distracted while he dug and sniffed the corner of the yard. Peg crouched next to him, inspecting the mysterious patch of garden. When she lifted up a rotting two-by-four from under a blanket of moldy leaves, the dog hopped left and right around her.

"Okay, good grief. I don't see any–" No sooner were the words out of her mouth, than a toad the size of a bowling ball jumped out at her. "Ahhhhh," she screamed and lurched back. The dog barked excitedly and readied himself for the attack pounce.

"Nipper, come here." Peg grabbed his collar. "No. No." She was no match for the superhuman strength of the dog. She fell backward, gripping the empty collar as her hindquarters hit the ground with considerable force. The dog flew through the air in direct pursuit of the humongous prehistoric creature.

"What eez going on?" The do-ragged yard guy ran over to see about the commotion.

"A giant frog… it jumped out at me. My dog has it. He won't let go." Peg crawled toward the dog who had latched onto the slimy, camouflaged toad.

"Get zee shovel," the man screamed to his emaciated worker who had joined the group. The thin man ran to the truck and grabbed the large metal shovel from the flatbed and threw it to the boss. "Get out of zee way. Get your dog away from zee frog. Zee frog can kill heem."

"KILL? Did you say KILL?" Peg scrambled in an effort to seize Nipper by the back legs, but he was too fast. The dog jumped sideways then up in the air, then back the other way – a whirling dervish, unable to be restrained. The gaunt man planted himself in the middle of the fray. Leaping like a gazelle, the man leg-locked the dog with his scrawny limbs, while catching hold of the dog's head. Like a lion tamer, he pried open the dog's mouth, forcing the behemoth frog to plunk on the ground. As soon as the frog hit the dirt, the boss raised the shovel above his head. With the precision of a master executioner – eyes focused and muscles taut – the weapon fell with deadly intent. Squash.

"Ahhh. I'm gonna be sick." Peg was sure she saw detached frog eyes stuck to the side of the white picket fence. She shook her hands, thinking that toad goop might have landed on her.

"No time for zat now. Get zee hose," the boss barked as he picked up the dog with one arm, carrying the 50-pound animal to the spigot. The skinny guy uncoiled the hose, turned on the water and, without any instruction at all, shoved the end of the hose into the dog's mouth. The boss man gripped the dog's head as the water squirted around Nipper's lips, teeth and tongue. The dog gagged and gurgled while struggling to escape but the boss's grip was too tight.

"What are you doing? You're drowning my dog." Peg grabbed the hose and yanked it. The hose slipped through the skinny man's fingers, but he grabbed it back just in time to commence a wet and wild tug of war with Peg. The spurting rubber tube seemed to take on a life of its own as it back-and-forthed between the two rivals.

"Zee frog was poisonous. We're *saving* your dog." With one arm controlling the frantic pet, the boss used the other arm to take back the hose and shove it into the dog's mouth. The helper, who was soaked to his bonyness, gave Peg a dirty look and helped his boss continue to flush out the dog's mouth.

"Poisonous frog? Oh my God. Nipper, are you okay?" Peg pet the dog as the water shot out of his mouth, showering the group as they stood close.

"Ee will be fine. You just need to watch eem. We caught eet in time." The boss put down the stunned dog. Peg placed the collar around the dog's neck, tightened it and held it fast while the dog flapped his ears, spraying yet more water in Peg's face.

"Zat is a bufo toad. Zee skin is very poisonous to dogs. Eet can even kill a human if zee skin should get een zee mouth."

"My God. Killer frogs in my own yard." Peg shuddered. "Thank you, thank you, thank you, for saving my dog. I don't know what I would have done. I didn't know about the bufo toad. I'm Peg, by the way." She wiped off her muddy hand on her hip and offered it to him. She shook his hand and felt the firm, calloused grip.

She looked at herself in the house window reflection: hair wet and unruly, shirt wet and stained with God-knows-what, muffin top wet and still there – *what a mess.* "I just moved here. I mean *we* just moved here... my husband and me. He's not here... he's in Cuba. He'll be back soon I'm sure. Anyway, we don't have bufo toads in Chicago. Too cold to mutate probably. We have tiny regular frogs... little cute guys... ribbit, ribbit... no poison or death."

"I'm Pierre and zis eez Charles, my elper." He pointed over to Charles, who had already gone back to the frog-murder site and was cleaning up the gelatinous body parts. He shoveled the big pieces into his wheelbarrow then rinsed off the ground and fence with the mangled hose. Charles glanced up at the introduction then continued on with his work.

"Zee scorpions are bad zis year. And of course zee iguanas will bite a dog eef cornered. Zee iguana poop will not kill you. But eet is deesgusting." He looked up into the large tree overhead and Peg followed his gaze. "Eef you want, I will kill zem with my gun if I see zem in your tree."

"Oh no. No more killing today. Thanks though." Peg eyed the gun rack on the back of his truck. "Scorpions too?"

This is hell... I'm in hell.

She crouched down to wrap her arms around Nipper. "Do you think I should take him to a vet?"

"Ee should be okay. Eef he starts to foam at the mouth, zen you need to take eem in." Pierre turned to pet the dog, who seemed suspicious at first, but once he realized the hose was nowhere near, he rubbed his wet face against Pierre's pant leg. "Eez a good dog. Eef you need my help, you can call me. Ze name eez on zee truck." He pointed to the vehicle. The sign said PIERRE. "Come on, Charles, let's go."

"Thanks again. Really, I owe you. Thank you so much."

Pierre nodded his head and pointed to the truck sign again.

Peg watched Charles load the wheelbarrow and shovel onto the flatbed. He climbed up next to the equipment and sat on the trailer, perfectly concealed by the assortment of sticks and twigs.

Pierre pulled himself up into the driver's seat, waved a brawny arm and drove off.

Soaking wet – covered in mud – scared to death – on a beautiful day in Key West, Peg and Nipper locked themselves inside the house. Peg decontaminated the dog's mouth with sterile wipes then rewarded him with treats. When he needed to go out, she kept his leash tight, carefully inspecting every step they took, looking both up and down.

By nightfall, they snuggled each other close on the couch.

The room smelled of disinfectant and bacon bits – and empty wine bottles.

Out of Her Element in the Elements

> *Text message from Trudy to Peg*
>
> `He's a total butt wipe.`

Trudy's text came through on Peg's phone. Peg smiled when she saw her friend's name pop up.

> *Text message from Peg to Trudy*
>
> `He's doing the charitable thing.`

> *Text message from Trudy to Peg*
>
> `Yeah, I bet - whatever. Well U GOTTA GET OUT THERE AND TRY SOMETHING NEW.`

> *Text message from Peg to Trudy*
>
> `I know. Are u yelling at me?`

> *Text message from Trudy to Peg*
>
> `NO. I have no idea how the all-caps got`

stuck. But you should sign up for something. Make an effort in that godforsaken place.

Text message from Peg to Trudy

I AM. I'm leaving in a minute for Mass.

Text message from Trudy to Peg

Yikes, okay, well I guess that's a start.

Text message from Peg to Trudy

Looks like a nice church. I'll let u know how it goes. Text u later.

Text message from Trudy to Peg

Umm, it's a Catholic church. It's the same wherever u are.

Text message from Peg to Trudy

That's exactly what I'm hoping for, but I'm not convinced it will be the same. LOL.

Why did I put "Laughing out Loud"? I should have put:

CATIAD (Crying And Turning Into A Drunk) Or…
SAH (Sweaty and Hot) Or…
EHCKU (Everything Here Can Kill You).

Peg filled several rubber dog toys with peanut butter and scattered them around the house. "I'll be back soon." Peg consoled the dog, his tail wagging as he settled in on the nearest delicious treat.

The church was a half-mile walk, but Peg started to wilt at step number ten. Her newly washed, blow-dried and curled hair forgot all the effort that Peg had made and turned instantly into frizz. Her armpits produced sweat rings that changed the underarm color of her light blue dress to dark purply yellow.

Note to self – never wear cotton ever again.

She felt her soaked white panties clinging to her dress as she walked, creating an X-rated wet stain.

Maybe I should take them off. Right… great idea. Take off your underwear as you are heading into church. That's not weird. Also, then you'll be dripping out of your dress… impressive.

The church was light and open, suggestions of the sea throughout the decor. People filed in as the ushers offered seats to the groups. Peg declined a seat, deciding that a sweaty buttocks imprint on her backside was not what she wanted the sanctuary to see as she went up for communion. Plus, she might be able to let the dress breathe if she stood and swayed a bit. The ushers were insistent, however, since there were many empty seats and no reason for a lone woman to be standing during Mass. The stern usher guided her to a spot next to a Latino family and a couple of over-sunned tourists. Staring at the church bulletin, Peg pretended not to know where the "squish" sound came from when she sat down on the wooden pew.

The Mass was the same, praise God, and she took comfort in the ritual of the words. Closing her eyes, she imagined she was back in her old parish – dark, cool, familiar. She relaxed and her sweat glands took a production break.

In a serene, baritone voice, the priest said, "Now it's time for the intentions. As we begin hurricane season, we pray to Sister Gabriel to keep us safe from devastating hurricanes."

What?

Peg looked up to see if anyone else had lifted their heads from prayer.

Hurricane season has started? Who the heck is Sister Gabriel and what powers does she have?

Sweat glands back on the job, she worried her way up to communion as she held her hands behind her back, hoping that her blotted butt-cheek stains were not a reality. The priest placed the host on her tongue. Close up, she could see the outline of his Tommy Bahama shirt under his light colored vestments. His huarache sandals looked downright biblical.

He raised his arm to give the final blessing, "I invite all of you to the grotto, located in the church gardens, to say an *additional* prayer to Sister Gabriel. The Mass has ended. Go in peace." After Peg *Amened*, she determined it would be a good idea to go visit the Sister's grotto for the second prayer.

Filing out of the pew, Peg followed other parishioners around the side of the white basilica to a lush shaded garden. While the crowd peeled off to the parking lot, she stopped in front of the statue of Sister Louis Gabriel. She bowed her head and began to pray.

Dear Sister Gabriel – thank you for your hurricane protection...

The sunburned tourist positioned himself next to her and cleared his throat. Peg side-eyed him with semi-closed lids.

I'm grateful for your...

The man nudged Peg. "Looks kinda like the Emperor from *Star Wars*, don't she?" He pointed at the statue of Sister Gabriel.

Doesn't this random stranger see that I'm praying? Does everyone talk to everyone here?

She ignored him, but then thought Jesus would have wanted her to be nicer, so she lifted her head. The statue's white alabaster face looked out from under a black granite hood. Feeling it was bad form to make fun of a nun, especially a hurricane-protection nun, in the middle of hurricane season, Peg replied, "I don't see the resemblance." She closed her eyes, hoping the man would take the hint.

The man placed his sunglasses on top of his flushed head and his reading glasses on the tip of his nose. "Says here that the Sister witnessed three major hurricanes. Since she put up this grotto in 1922, the island's been safe. As long as the grotto stands, Key West is protected," he read from a travel book in a raspy voice.

Peg stepped closer to the altar. Awed by the power of this protection, she genuflected and crossed herself as she entered the cave-like grotto. Desiring to feel the physical presence of Sister Gabriel's blessing, she caressed the cool rock wall, amazed by the history and significance.

It's like a magical force field. Kinda like the blue front porch.

Leaning in to get a better look, her purse clunked into the wall and loosened a craggy rock. *Thud,* the rock hit the dirt.

Uh-oh.

She turned her head left and right to see if anyone was watching her.

The oblivious tourist continued reading: "Says here that the hurricane of 1846 brought a lot of interred bodies back up. The hurricane also brought high winds, and a number of corpses ended up in the branches of the trees around town. That's somethin' I wouldn't wanna see." He shook his head in a "no siree."

Peg scooped up the rock and hid it in her sweaty armpit, trying not to enjoy its coolness against her skin.

"Well, have a nice day." The man rearranged his glasses, closed his book and walked away.

"Bye." Peg clamped her armpit tight as she waved. Waiting to make sure that he was out of sight, she reached over and shoved the rock into the wall. It slipped back out.

Damn. It's too sweaty. Uh-oh... did I just say the word "damn" in a holy shrine?

She crammed it with more force and it held.

"Praise God." She exhaled.

She knelt in place, closed her eyes and prayed. *Dear God, Jesus and Sister Gabriel, sorry for saying a bad word in your shrine… and also…*

Then it started.

Plop.

Plop, plop.

Plop, plop, plop, plop.

Peg opened an eye.

What? How can this be happening? I said I was sorry.

She crawled to the wall in a frenzied attempt to replace the fallen rocks in the honeycomb-like openings. In unsuccessful little-Dutch-boy moves, the more she put back, the more rocks loosened and fell in an avalanche-like plunge.

I've doomed the island. Gotta get outta here…

Fueled by panic attack and adrenaline, covered in coral dust and sweat, she sprang from the cave. She bolted past the lone garden dweller and a teenage girl absorbed in primping and pouting for the perfect selfie.

Oh my God. So sorry, Sister. Oh my God, oh my God, oh my God.

As fast as her wobbly legs would take her, she ran out of the churchyard, through the hot city streets and into her house. Barging through the door, gasping for breath, she leaned over the kitchen counter. The dog barely acknowledged her as he started in on rubber-peanut-butter toy number three.

The phone in her purse buzzed. Peg ratted through the purse contents to locate the device.

Oh maybe it's Clark. Maybe he's coming back sooner. Please let this be him.

Text message from Trudy to Peg

`How'd it go?`

Trudy's text beeped in.

Peg's shoulders slumped as her wet, shaky finger swiped the

screen. She texted back in a sad–annoyed–defensive–freaked–out way.

Text message from Peg to Trudy

What do you mean?

Text message from Trudy to Peg

The Mass. How was it? The same, right?

Peg pushed the microphone icon and yelled the text message.

Text message from Peg to Trudy

No, not remotely the same. I developed X-rated sweat stains on my dress on the way to church, then Sister Gabriel promised to keep hurricanes away as long as her grotto stands, and I couldn't get a sweaty armpit rock to fit back in the wall, so the grotto fell down, and now there will be corpses hanging from trees.

Trudy texted back right away.

Text message from Trudy to Peg

Ha ha. Your autocorrect is cracking me up. Uh-oh. Got a call coming in. ttyl.

Hitting the microphone button with greater force this time, Peg screamed into the phone.

Text message from Peg to Trudy

```
This is NOT autocorrect. This is REAL. I
might be PERSONALLY RESPONSIBLE for the next
ARMAGEDDON. Does that sound like it can be
corrected BY MY PHONE?
```

Peg shook her phone then paced around the kitchen in an effort to calm herself.

Pull yourself together.

Peg hoped that the shivers down her spine were due to the air conditioning refrigerating her wet dress. Nipper paced behind her, carrying an empty rubber toy carcass in his mouth. Deciding that he had been in the house long enough, he stopped by the back door and barked.

Peg jumped.

My God. I'm a nervous wreck.

Nipper would be a good distraction. "Okay," she said to the dog. "Hang on, I'll change into dry clothes and we'll go." Taking deep cleansing breaths while she walked the five steps to the bedroom, she maneuvered around the furniture while trying not to look at the unused side of the king-size bed. The dresser's close proximity to the bed restricted the drawers to a two-inch opening – enough for her to thread her fingers through the top and grab garments without getting a visual on the capture.

Fine. Black underwear, red sports bra, jean shorts and University of Illinois tee shirt. At least they are dry… well… not exactly dry… damp… which is like the definition of dry down here.

She opened a kitchen closet door and tossed the *first* sweaty outfit of the day into the stacked washing machine. The kitchen calendar had ten days crossed off.

The rest of today and five more to go… that will be two weeks. I can do it.

Leaving the house, Nipper twirled his way to the sidewalk – high on peanut butter and outside air. Pulse steadying as she watched the happy dog, she smiled. "You have the right attitude, my friend."

They made their way along their regular route, the dog making sure to pee on everything that had ever been peed on since the beginning of time, with a particular affinity for newspaper dispensers. While waiting for the dog to exert his island dominance, a chatting couple walked toward them on the sidewalk. The woman turned toward her partner and laughed at something the man said. He hugged her around the waist and she kissed him.

I really miss Clark…

Peg's eyes welled and she turned her face down as they passed by and greeted her.

Stop it… clearing my brain… positive energy…

In the midst of her inner fight, she noticed a flyer attached to a fence. She flattened the curled edges of the paper against the chain-link to read it.

Feeling stressed and out of sorts?
Come and join us on Mondays!
Yoga – Key West style
Enjoy the calming beauty of the water
And the healing benefits of Yoga.
Namaste – find your drishti – PBY

A voice behind her took her by surprise. "You should come. I go to this class every week."

Peg turned to see the man and the chihuahua from 12 days and 22 hours ago. The chihuahua pressed its nose on the ground next to Nipper, vying for ownership of the same square inch of the fence. Even outfitted in full ballerina regalia, the little dog fit perfectly underneath the vizsla's legs. From above they looked like a freakish circus animal – four legs, two heads and a tutu.

"Oh, hi. This is Lulu, right?" Peg reached down to pet the

miniature creature, then hesitated, remembering those razor-sharp teeth.

"Yes, that's the princess." He bowed and rolled his arms out dramatically toward the dog. "And I'm Randolph. I live down the street." Randolph held his hand out over the sparkly pink dog stroller. "She couldn't wait to get out of her chariot to see your dog. It's an honor. She isn't like that with everyone. Or anyone as a matter of fact." He smiled with symmetrical dimples.

Peg wiped her hand on her tee shirt then held it out. "Sorry, can't stop sweating. Nice to meet both of you. I'm Peg and this is Nipper. We live around the corner." The big dog lifted his head to greet the man, then resumed sniffing, having lost considerable ground to the chihuahua when he left his post.

"You should come." Randolph pointed to the weather-worn flyer.

"I could really use it. I've had quite a morning. I went to church... and... we prayed... and—"

"Great. I'll pick you up," Randolph interrupted. "It's the neighborly thing to do. What house is it?"

"Oh. No. You don't have to do that. Really."

"We pride ourselves on our friendliness here in Key West. So. Don't be silly. Of course I'll come and get you. Give me your address."

"The white one with the wood bench on the front porch. But I don't know. I'm not great at yoga."

"I *won't* take no for an answer. I'll be there at 8.45am. Hmm. The white house with the front porch? I *know* that house. The haunted house tour bus stops there. I always wondered what they had to say."

"Well... uh..."

"No arguing." Randolph scooped up Lulu who growled as he dropped her in the buggy. He waved with his elbow as he wrangled the dog. "See you tomorrow. Lulu, stay in your seat, you barbarian, or I'll zip up the lid." The multicolored ribbons woven in the stroller's wheel spokes matched the geometrical design across the lid, and the silver rhinestones across the handle added that extra bit of bling. The contents of the stroller fought its captivity. Randolph's phony scolding grew faint as they rolled away.

"What was I thinking?" Peg yanked on the leash to get her dog away from the most interesting and fascinating of all fence posts.

Gotta get out of this. I'll say I have a horrible rash… that covers my entire body… not just the underboob rash, which is real and will NOT go away. No. You need to do something besides sit in the house. Plus, this might help relieve your stress. Really? How is seeing my own fat and cellulite flop around going to help relieve stress? Will give new meaning to cow pose.

Battling herself back into the house, she unleashed the dog and walked straight to her laptop. Seconds later, she jumped when Trudy's face popped up on the screen.

"Oh. You scared me. But it is good to see your face." Peg's own face looked anxious and red.

"What is the matter? Last I heard you were going to Mass. Then I got those crazy text messages. Are you okay?"

"No. I'm not." In one long and unpunctuated breath, Peg filled Trudy in on the events of the morning and afternoon.

"Whoa. Whoa. I think you're hyperventilating." Trudy held up her hand to the screen. "First of all, that grotto-slash-hurricane business is nonsense. I'm looking up hurricanes now. Google says that hurricanes start as storms off the sub-Saharan desert. They have nothing to do with a 90-year-old pile of rocks."

"But–"

"Second of all. You are going to the yoga class with, what's his name again? Randolph? I mean normally I'd run a criminal background check on the guy, but he's got a chihuahua for God's sake. He's probably not a serial killer. A chihuahua means that he's okay. Plus, he sounds nice and he sounds like he could be a friend. So, tomorrow morning, get your ass out of the pity party and into your yoga pants."

"Okay. You're right. I'm not sure they still fit. I think they're from 1990."

"Of course I'm right. And, yoga pants are stretchy. They'll fit. When did you say your loser husband gets back?"

"Trudy," Peg reprimanded.

"Sorry. When does Clark get home?"

"On Friday." Peg's face lit up.

"Such an–"

"I miss him." Peg fanned away the tears with hands.

Trudy rolled her eyes behind her glasses. "I don't miss him, but I do miss you. Call me tomorrow night. We can video chat with the dogs. Tucker is sleeping now."

"Okay. Bye."

"Go to yoga."

"I will. Bye."

Follow up email from Trudy

```
Just in case:
How to escape from the trunk of a car:
Pull trunk release. ("If" car has one.)
Some cars have ways to get out through the
back seat. (Make sure that kidnapper is NOT
in the back seat with you.)
  Push out brake lights so you can wiggle
fingers through the hole. (Wiggle vigor-
ously.)
What does the guy look like and what are your
final wishes?
```

And so it turned out that Sunday was not a day of rest after all.

All Keyed Up

Email to Trudy

I think *I'll be fine*, but in response to your request, Randolph will most likely be wearing a yoga outfit. He has superb dimples.
Oh and I wouldn't pet his Chihuahua Lulu. She bites.
In the case of my untimely demise, please drive down here as fast as possible to get Nipper. You know he can't handle flying. And most importantly, I want to be buried in Alaska (sorry, high maintenance). I'd like my skin to feel cold, dry air for its last time on earth.

Peg sat on the floor facing her dog. "I think I have everything covered. You have lots of food and water." She pressed her nose against his as she spoke. "You'll be fine and I'll be very Zen when I return."

She found her dusty yoga mat in a box with the Christmas ornaments. The yoga pants saw their first daylight in a quarter of a century.

AH OOGA. AH OOGA. AH OOGA. AH OOGA.

What the…?

Peg opened the front door and saw Randolph driving a converted golf cart with a Flintstone-esque retro-fit.

"Hiya, Peg." Randolph smiled. He squeezed the rubber ball attached to the horn on the dashboard. The giant tusks mounted to the front of the vehicle magnified the sound. AH OOGA.

Peg smiled back. She bounced down the steps with her yoga mat and her purse, and stepped into the open-air vehicle.

Randolph turned off the golf-cart radio as she got in. "Oh, big news. Did you hear about the grotto? It's toast. They just talked about it on the radio."

Peg blanched.

"Not sure I believe all of that – but lots of people do." He shrugged his shoulders. "Anyway, que sera sera."

Peg sat stock straight, her face frozen in panic behind her sunglasses.

The grotto... on the news–

"Helloo, earth to Peg." Randolph AH OOGA'd the horn. "I *asked* you if you like my wheels?"

"Wheels? Oh. Yes, very... um... *Neanderthal.*" Cold sweat dripped down her neck.. "Ah – Thank you for picking me up. I've been looking forward to this," she lied.

"You're not going to need that mat, honey," Randolph said over the sounds of the traffic.

"Oh. Okay. They use their own?" Peg questioned.

"You're cracking me up right now." His dimples showed off their magnificence. He pushed down the gas pedal and after a long pause the wheels began to move at a snail's pace. "It's electric. I'm a conservationist."

Peg nodded. "That's good, but why don't I need–?"

Randolph waved her off. "Look at this diamond," he said, pointing to the stud in his ear. "No blood diamonds for me. I'm a pacifist too." The earring caught the sunlight and tiny specks of color disco-danced around him. "But I gotta have my bling." He giggled.

Peg laughed and began to relax.

Randolph took his local celebrity status in his stride. The "whoo whoos" and "yabba dabba doos" from passersby were returned with a poised royal wave and a stately grin. Peg was getting used to seeing people and pets on scooters in Key West. The bigger dogs rode on the footrest in-between the human's legs. The smaller dogs sat alongside on the seat. No one wore helmets except, sometimes, the dogs. A man (and his dog) stopped his (their) scooter next to the caveman mobile and chatted amiably with Randolph. When the light turned green, the dog decided to make a leap for the stuffed bones dangling decoratively from the rearview mirror of the golf cart. Peg tensed up, thinking that the dog was going to land in her lap, but without missing a beat, the scooter-man nabbed the dog in midair, returned the dog to his seat and motored away.

Randolph was unperturbed by the commotion. "Doesn't the ocean look beautiful today? Who wouldn't want to live on this two-by-four-mile island? Its history is so romantic – pirates then wreckers. Those reefs are a ship's nightmare. They stretch from Miami all the way down the Gulf." He arm-swept toward the water. "Lots-o-people made lots-o-money off those shipwrecks." Randolph looked at Peg while he was talking.

"Uh huh… uhhh. Watch out!" Peg pointed to the oncoming traffic.

Randolph swerved the Flintstones mobile back into its lane and continued his history lesson. "A lot of mansions are decorated with stuff from the ships. You should go see some of them – marble floors, grand pianos, you name it. There was talk that lanterns were put on the reef in the wrong place to cause wrecks. Thank goodness – because the island got some fabulous artifacts." He pretended a sinister laugh. "Just kidding. But not really."

At the stoplight, he braked inches from the car in front of them. Peg closed her eyes under her sunglasses. Randolph continued his history lesson. "Roosevelt built a road down here because the railroad went *buh bye* in 1938. You know. Hurricane."

Peg cringed.

"Then we got the '60s and '70s with the hippies and the shrimpers living side by side, then the navy base closed and *finally* the '80s and '90s when the gays came into town and renovated the ramshackle houses. Peace on the island at last." He turned his head to the right. "You got all that?"

Peg nodded her agreement, while looking straight ahead at the road, wishing that Randolph would do the same. A pickup truck with the windows blackened out drove dangerously close to the back of the golf cart, revved its engines, then blew past them in a giant puff of exhaust.

"Hey, watch out, asshole." Randolph coughed through the smoke and thrust out his middle finger.

So much for pacifism.

"How fast does your... ummm... car... uh... cart... uh vehicle go?" Peg noticed that there was quite a traffic jam behind them.

"Oh, she can do 35 if I open her up. And, BTW her name is Betty."

"Betty. Okay." Peg patted the dashboard. She scooted to her left as, one by one, bicycles passed them – whooshing inches from her right ear. "You should be a tour guide. How long have you lived in Key West?"

"I'm a *Fresh Water Conch* – that means I've lived in Key West over seven years. If you're born and raised here, you're a plain old *Conch*. I don't like to give classifications to people, but no one asked *my* opinion." Randolph pursed his lips.

Turning right off of Route 1, Betty snuggled into a shaded parking spot, preventing future third-degree buttock burns. Peg reached once more for her yoga mat. "You sure that I won't need this?"

Randolph shook his head. "Positive."

Peg tossed the mat back onto the seat and walked alongside Randolph. "So where is this place? Kind of looks like a marina to me."

"It's up here. And it's a marina too."

"Hmm, so where is the studio?" Peg asked as they approached a group of people standing around getting instructions of some sort.

"Studio? What do you mean?"

"Like... where we do the yoga?"

"Oh, honey. This is paddleboard yoga."

Peg stopped in her tracks. "What is paddleboard yoga?" she hissed. "I can't do paddleboard yoga!"

"Didn't you read the flyer? It clearly said PBY. You do have your bathing suit on, right?"

Peg peered down at her yoga pants. "No."

Randolph eyed her body. "Well, you can go with your spandex on. Lots of people wear yoga clothes to protect from the sun." Unfazed by her freaked-out-ness, he lifted her purse off of her shoulder. "I'll lock this up," he said and pushed her forward. The instructor handed her a seven-foot-long paddle.

"I didn't know what PBY meant. I thought it was like a breathing thing or meditation. Not doing yoga on a surfboard in the ocean. I'm not a great swimmer."

He shook his head. "You're not swimming, doll. It's a paddleboard, not a surfboard. It's stable. You'll be fine. Take off your shoes." Randolph hustled her to the line of class members waiting for their boards and tossed her sandals in the lobster trap that served as a shoe repository. The life jackets were bungeed to the board to be used in an emergency, most of them dry and crusty from lack of use. Randolph wrenched one from a board and plunked it over her head. Fastening the straps around her body, he nudged her toward the edge of the dock.

Like soldiers in a drum line, ten tanned, fit students walked onto their boards. All of them wore bikinis, including the men. One by one they turned then knelt at attention to face the instructor, paddles held across their laps like samurai swords.

"I can't do this." Peg looked for an escape route but Randolph's tall body blocked her view.

"Yes, you can." Randolph guided her toward the board, the front of which was securely docked – only the tail end touched the water.

"No, I can't."

But it was too late – no way out – no escape. Peg tentatively stepped onto the board, dropped immediately to her knees and crawled to the middle. As she turned to kneel, her life jacket pushed up past her face and around her ears forming a moldy, smelly back brace. Yanking down the bottom of the jacket in order to gain some mobility and breathing room, she sat up on her knees. Randolph was next to her sitting cross-legged on his board with his eyes shut.

Okay, so maybe we just stay docked. I might be able to do it if I take off the life jacket… and I might not die without a life jacket since we are technically still on land. Deep breath in –

No sooner had she expanded her lungs than she felt the board move.

"Sit back on your haunches, miss. I'll push your board off the dock." The instructor had a pink and green tattoo of an elephant/human rippling across her muscular back.

"Wait, where are we going? I thought that we could stay here." Peg was thrown backward on her heels as the board moved into the water – the life preserver returned to strangle status. The board wobbled unevenly as she sat up, fending off strangulation.

My life preserver is killing me.

"Grab your paddle, Peg, and do this–" Randolph was in the water and demonstrated how to paddle while kneeling. "As soon as you get the hang of it, you can stand up." He popped up to standing on his board. He gracefully glided over to her.

The instructor's bossy/calm voice lilted over the water. "Paddle yourselves out and meet the class by the mangroves outside of the marina. I'll hand out the anchors there."

"No way. All the way out there? I'll never make it." Peg glanced past the boats in the marina. It was a solid 100 yards to the mangroves.

"If you want, you can stay low on the board and paddle until you get used to it." Randolph swirled around her in circles.

"I'm going to fall off." Peg saw the fish darting beneath her in the clear water.

"If you fall off you get back on. That's the worst that can happen."

No, the worst thing that can happen is that I drown and Clark has to live out his adventure by himself… wait… that's kinda happening already… maybe I'm dead… and I'm in –

Jolted back into the real world, Peg saw a six-foot shadow swimming under her board, then another one, then another one. She froze in fear. "Oh my God. What are those? Tell me those are not sharks." She got on her hands and knees, eyes fixated on the monster shadows lurking below.

"Those are tarpon, Peg, not sharks. They hang out by the marina looking for leftover fish parts. They won't bite yellow-bellied humans, so you're safe." Randolph's dimples deepened in a smile as he paddled in line with the other boarders heading for the mangroves. He turned to check on Peg's progress.

White-knuckled, on her hands and knees, with her life jacket covering half of her head, she remained paralyzed. She drifted toward the idling fishing boats, loaded with tourists and ready to start out.

"Peg. Sit up and paddle, or the boats will run you over." Randolph broke from the ranks and stroked toward her.

Jolted out of her daze by the threat of engine decapitation, she sat back to kneeling. She spread her thighs out to increase balance and paddled. Surprising herself, she moved forward and in the right direction.

"You go, girl. Keep going." Randolph pumped his arm. "Whoo, whoo." He steered behind her and they made their way to the mangroves.

The green leaves and vines jutted out of the water in mini shrubbery islands. Sweat stung Peg's eyes as they paddled up to the other people who were standing on their boards and chatting sociably. They greeted Randolph with a friendly "hello" and introduced themselves to Peg.

The zero-body-fat instructor floated next to them and circled the group as she spoke. "I'm Kalinda and I'll be guiding you through today. We'll head out into the mangroves and anchor in a beautiful cove for our practice. I invite you to follow me in body and mind." When she turned, the eye of the elephant head tattoo stared from her sculpted scapula. Her board levitated above the water, the paddle barely making a ripple. The ten other class members all had similar rippleless exits.

"What? We have to paddle more?"

"Why don't you try to stand up? Honestly, it's easier," Randolph begged with paddle in armpit and hands in prayer.

Sensing Randolph's frustration, not wanting to be left alone in the mangroves only to be found drifting off Cuba in a reverse commuting way, Peg placed her feet in a sumo squat. Slowly, using all of her quad strength – holding her paddle in tightrope-wire-walker fashion – she rose. "I'm up."

"Don't overthink it. Let's go."

Once up, gravity assisted her life jacket in taking its appropriate spot on her body. Rivers of pooled sweat trickled down her yoga pants. She paddled one side and then the other. The warm Caribbean breeze pushed her from behind as her toes curled in a pre-cramp effort to keep her upright. The strong current carried the board.

I'm doing it. It's okay… like a lazy river ride. Boy, if only Trudy could see me now.

"Look around you. It's a beautiful day. Relax." Randolph leaned against his paddle, letting the flow of the water guide the board.

Peg glanced up for a brief moment but not wanting to jinx the good karma, returned to focusing on her balance. Perhaps using too much focus, she failed to notice that the group was already meditating, cross-legged on their boards with their anchors in the water. With a little less focus, she might have noticed she was coming in to meet the group at a fairly good clip, and her board had found a strong current.

Ramming speed.

When she did look up, it was too late. "Watch out," she shrieked in an un-yoga-like manner as she careened into the circle, taking out two of the better meditators. "I'm sorry. I'm so sorry. I couldn't stop."

The wet yogis swam back to their boards. They both said that it was okay but that was only because it was a yoga class and cursing was frowned upon. Kalinda made some comment about love and acceptance. She paddled toward Peg to hand her an anchor. Upon reaching for it, Peg crawled too far to the front of her board and the weight of the anchor sent her plunging into the water headfirst. Her (now vacant) board shot backward out of the water at rocket-launch speed, with a direct path to the wet yogis who had just remounted their boards. Back into the water they fled, successfully averting contact with the projectile paddleboard. The untied anchor plunked on the bottom in a puff of silt. Peg flailed and clawed at her life vest, causing a ruckus of waves until she realized she could stand on the sea bottom. All of the other class participants were belly-down on their boards, surf style – the tidal waves of churned water sloshing over their backs as they held on for dear life.

Kalinda paddled through the cyclone to retrieve Peg's board, which had gained a considerable amount of distance. Requesting that Peg swim out to her, she anchored it a safe ten feet outside of the inner yoga circle.

"Hop back on your board now, Peg, and we'll get started," Kalinda said as if her chakra was out of whack.

"Thank you. I'm so sorry. I'm from Chicago. We don't do this there... water is frozen," Peg gasped as she guppied over to her board, trying not to touch the mushy sea floor.

"Pull yourself back onto your board," Kalinda said, in a not-so-nicey tone.

Peg held the side of the board and, with a big kick, hoisted herself up to chest level. Once there, the life jacket moisture and the rubbery footing on the paddleboard created a congealed bond. "I'm stuck. The jacket's stuck." Peg tugged, squirmed and wiggled but her legs remained in the water with her butt facing up and bent over the board.

"Pull harder with your arms." Kalinda positioned her board next to Peg's and sat with legs dangling in the water. She leaned over and grasped the shoulders of Peg's jacket and, using her feet as leverage against the board, Kalinda heaved. Peg's unsticking was a dramatic success as she careened over the board and into the water on the other side, sending Kalinda into a spectacular backflip.

Wet and bedraggled, Kalinda summoned her namaste and her board and swam until she was behind Peg in the water. "Let's try this again. I'll hoist you up."

Alternately inhaling and ingesting salt water, Peg coughed but obeyed and held the board with her arms. "On the count of three... one, two, three."

Kalinda hugged the backs of Peg's thighs and with the strength of thousands of Ganeshes hoisted Peg up. Like a fish out of water, Peg flailed until she was flat on her board. Chest heaving, the soaking wet life jacket leaked water out to the rhythm of her breath.

Paddleboarding? More like waterboarding.

Kalinda lifted herself onto her own board in one swift motion and paddled back to the group. Prostrate on her board, Peg was acutely aware of the class sitting uneasily on their boards, each of them with one eye closed and one eye on her. "I invite us all to start with an easy down dog to stretch out our minds and give us new perspective." One by one, each yogi planted feet and hands firmly on their boards and stuck their buttocks in the air. "I invite us to take in a cleansing breath."

Kalinda lowered herself out of down dog to assess the class's form. She eyed Peg who hadn't moved.

"Peg, are you going to try it?" Kalinda queried. Her jaw clenched as she spoke.

"No. Declining invitation."

"Maybe just on your hands and knees?" Kalinda baby-talked.

Peg felt like a dog, all right. "No... not moving." She remained resolutely face down on her board.

"Come on, doll. You can do it." This from Randolph, who was upside down, staring at her through his legs.

Don't be a quitter. Nobody likes a quitter.

Hearing the collective belly breathing of the class, Peg sighed and willed herself to:

Lift her head.

Lift her stomach.

Lift her legs.

On hands and knees, she swayed from side to side, as the water rocked the board.

"Now lift your tushy," Randolph encouraged.

Jeez, tushy, really? Is my grandmother here? Okay. Fine.

Lift her tushy.

I'm doing it... down dog on a paddleboard. I can't believe it.

Her world had literally been turned upside down. The crystal blue water traded places with the cloudless blue sky as she gazed between her legs. *Amazing.*

The hour went by with Kalinda suggesting a variety of poses. The class eagerly obliged. After down dog, however, Peg chose corpse pose. Face up, arms and legs splayed across the board, her clothing exuding damp dog. The sun beat down on her wet polyester creating salty perspiration.

Maybe one little sip of ocean water... so thirsty.

"Peg. Peg. Can you hear me?" Randolph straddled his own board and poked a finger into Peg's bicep.

"Hello, Granny." Peg's head lifted one inch off her board then fell back. Pinpricks of lights filled her vision. Her hands splashed the water in a flapping motion.

Randolph's voice sounded distorted in Peg's head. "I think she might be dehydrated. I'll tow her back to the dock."

Through ringing ears Peg could hear, "give her some water – she's not an attorney, is she?"

Randolph leaned in with his Thermos and squirted water into Peg's mouth.

"Thank you, bartender, but I think I've had enough... feeling woozy. Am I in Cuba yet?" Peg's words slurred.

Randolph hooked the anchor line to his own board and paddled himself and his albatross through the mangroves. Flat on her back, limbs dangling in the water, Peg sang off-tune, "Yo, ho, tow them away, the Lincoln Park Pirates are we." Then she said, "You wouldn't know that song... it's from Chicago... about the tow trucks... they tow everyone... it's cold there..."

Randolph turned around and yelled back to her, "What a hot mess you are."

"Smokin' hot... you know it, Grams."

Haints Go Marchin' In

"I'm fine. Really." Peg sat up on her couch as Randolph force-fed her water. She didn't remember the ride to her house from the marina or singing show tunes in Betty's back seat. "How did Lulu get here?" Lulu and Nipper were having a smell-fest.

"I picked her up during 'Singing in the Rain' but before 'When you're a Jet.'" Randolph re-soaked the wet paper towel for her forehead. "I have some bad news for you – you will never make it in showbiz."

Peg smiled and placed the cloth on her head. The room had stopped spinning and the Advil was beginning to do its job. "I don't think I know the words to those songs."

"You don't. Only the first line – over and over." He rolled his head in a circular motion.

"Thank you for saving me. That's never happened to me before. In Chicago–"

"I know. I know. It's cold in Chicago. I get it." Randolph threw his arms up in the air. "But," he softened, "you're welcome. I told you, Key West is a friendly town. We don't leave our paddle-boarders out in the mangroves to die. It's the kind of people we are." He put his hands on his hips and stuck out a proud rooster chest.

"So, Lulu and Nipper like each other." Peg pointed to the animals chasing a tennis ball across the wood floor. Lulu grabbed the prize and hot-dogged around Nipper, making sure to go under his legs – because she could.

The vizsla's 50 pounds in true body mass was no match for the chihuahua's 1,000 pounds of attitude. He couldn't take his eyes off of her – a combination of fear, admiration and, quite possibly, love.

"She is such a diva. I believe she's chosen your dog to be one of her followers. He must be worthy. Quite an honor actually." Randolph took Lulu by surprise when he scooped her up. She lashed out at him with impressive ferocity, and, had the ball not been in her mouth, she would have drawn blood. Randolph scolded, "What a tyrant. You'd never know that I'm her master. Little bitch."

Peg laughed at them. "She's boss. No doubt." Peg stood up to get her land legs. "Thanks so much. I know you must have better things to do today."

"Yes. I do need to take a shower. I burned a few extra calories on the paddle back to the dock." He rolled his neck and criss-crossed his forearms to massage his shoulders. Picking up a notepad and pen from the counter, he scribbled on the paper. "Here's our cell phone number if you need us. The neighborly Key Westers – right Lulu?" Lulu snapped at him. He held her at arm's distance as he walked out the door. "Take care. Buh bye."

"Bye and thanks again." Peg and Nipper watched them walk away – the queen and her minion.

"I need a shower and rest," Peg told her dog. "I hope that you're okay with that." The computer was open on the kitchen counter. The bold words "KIDNAPPING" and "ESCAPE" disappeared as she closed the cover.

Which is worse? Kidnapping or paddleboard yoga? I'd say it's a toss-up.

Peg cranked the cold water in the shower and stuck her wet hair in a knot on top of her head, à la Flintstones – *The Pebbles look. Perfect.* She shut the blinds and took one of Clark's old tee shirts out of the drawer.

Smells so good… so familiar…

The shirt felt cool and smooth over her sunburned, goose-pim-pled skin. Crawling into bed with her dog snuggled at her feet, the room embraced her. Peg coma-slept.

At midnight, the front porch started to glow. The blue ceiling strained against the pressure. The force field revealed its weakness when a shock of light blasted through the small patch of chipped blue paint. The phosphorescence separated into ghostly shapes that hesitated, then passed through the mahogany door and into Peg's bedroom. Encircling the sleeping woman in her bed, the apparitions began to speak.

"Stop thinking there is something going on. You're such a Negative Nancy," said the man in the flamboyant floppy hat, his legs crossed, as he floated through the air.

"No real man would leave his woman if there wasn't a little piece of chicken on the side," countered the brawny man with a dark gray beard and mustache, puffing on a cigar. The yellow smoke swirled around the room then dissipated into hazy nothingness.

Peg sat up with a start and pulled the sheets to her neck. The luminescent figures floated around her bed, staring down at her like she was the centerpiece of a conference table. She rubbed her eyes in disbelief.

"Ahhhhh." Peg squeaked a scream as she ducked under the covers.

OH MY GOD, it's true. There ARE HAINTS. They've come for me… the undead. Oh, why didn't I patch the paint on the front porch? Clark said he would do it even though I was being ridiculous. I was waiting for him to do it. Well, who is being ridiculous now? Maybe they won't see me. Maybe they'll leave me alone.

Peg attempted to quiet the echo of her heart pounding in her skull.

"Well, excuse me for having an opinion, Ernest. I know how much you like to be right. Answer this. Why would he bring her to Key West then, smarty-pants? Why wouldn't he leave her back in – wherever she's from?"

Peg muffled a terrified whimper.

"Now look what you've done. You've scared the poor creature."

"I am right, dammit. He wants to make sure he's always a man with a woman. Think about it, Tennessee, he drags her down here and then leaves practically before the next sunrise. His bell is tolling for someone else, I say."

A mewing, lilting voice came from the figure on the windowsill. "Are you two still bickering? Fighting to the death and beyond?" Peg peeked over the blanket and saw a six-toed cat licking her giant mitt of a paw as she glared at the men through unblinking eyes. Her tail swished back and forth like a bullfighter's whip.

"How'd you get in here, Snow White? The tin roof?" Tennessee Williams tee-heed at his own joke.

"Always self-promoting. The ultimate narcissist," Ernest Hemingway growled his words.

"Oh, puhleeeease. What about you? God's gift to the world of literature? At least I made my OWN money and didn't have to marry it." Tennessee crossed his arms dramatically.

"If you weren't already dead, I would box you across the room." Hemingway floated over with his ethereal fists in the air.

Snow White stopped her grooming. "Gentlemen. Gentlemen. Remember why we are here. Our frightened little mouse under the blankets needs our help. Let's get back on task." She drifted across the bed and positioned herself on top of Nipper, who remained curled up, fast asleep.

Peg kicked her feet in an unsuccessful attempt to wake the slumbering dog.

"Nipper, Nipper, can you hear me? Wake up for heaven's sake. Bark or do something."

"He can't hear you, dearie." Tennessee lifted the covers to see Peg curled in a human ball with her hands over her face. "Just because you have your eyes closed, doesn't mean we're not here. Peek-a-boo." He reached to lift one of her fingers away from her eyes.

She felt the wisp of a feather and twitched.

"Come on, woman. Sit up and pay attention." Hemingway's militaristic command shocked Peg into submission. She bolted upright.

Allowing herself to take attendance, Peg stammered, "Okay, Ernest Hemingway, writer, Key West, I get it."

She glanced to the other side of the bed. "Tennessee Williams, writer, Key West, I get that too. But, Hemingway's six-toed cat… don't get it… and… wish you would get off my dog." She made a shooing motion with her hand toward the end of the bed. The cat remained at her post, unfazed.

Peg turned her head to another figure in the corner of the room. "But who is–?"

Tennessee's melodic tone interrupted Peg's question. "Why do you think that your husband isn't here with you, love?"

"Well, he's in Cuba… on business–"

"Business, my ass. More like monkey business," Hemingway interrupted.

Snow White held up a stop-motion paw. "Now, now, Mr. Hemingway. Please let the homeowner speak."

"No… he is. He really is in Cuba doing consulting work." Peg's voice gained a bit of strength.

"We believe you, darlin', it's just that he left you… I don't know… so… all of a sudden. We want to believe you. We do." Tennessee's hat lolled up and down as he nodded his head.

Snow White kneaded the sleeping dog's back and purred, "We are here to help."

"Well, thanks for thinking of me, but I'm fine. I don't need help," Peg insisted.

"Don't look fine to me. Looks like you could use a stiff drink." Hemingway pointed his cigar in her direction.

"You'd look like you needed a drink too if you woke up to strange men in your room."

Tennessee turned his head sideways and feigned offense. "Who are you calling strange, madam?"

"Damn, I wish I *could* have a stiff drink." Ernest smacked his lips.

The cat interjected, "Let's not pussyfoot around here – even though, perhaps your husband is doing *just that*."

"No really, it's okay, he's coming back. People do this all the time now… it's not a problem that needs to be solved," Peg half-yelled.

"Of course. Of course, honey. We're on your side." Tennessee ghost patted her hand.

Other than a queasy stomach sensation, Peg was unable to feel the delicate, undead fingers as they appeared to touch her skin.

"She's delirious."

"She's in denial."

"That's why we're here."

The haints closed in on her.

"I don't have a side. I don't need your help. And who's that guy?" Peg pointed to the man in the corner.

The room became quiet as the group looked in his direction.

Tennessee and Ernest both shrugged.

Snow White broke the silence. "And who might you be?"

The quiet haint in the corner of the bedroom looked around, his eyes wide. "I'm Shel Silverstein."

Tennessee politely tipped the front of his oversized hat. "It's a pleasure to meet you, sir, but unfortunately, I believe you might be lost."

"Is this 1424 White Street?" Shel took out a see-through map from his shirt pocket.

"No, it's not." Hemingway looked annoyed.

"Ahh. My apologies, I saw a light in the attic, but I must have the wrong house." Shel snapped his fingers and disappeared.

Peg shot back under the covers and forced her eyes shut.

Echoes of the spectral voices grew dimmer.

"I can't abide tenderfoots."

"Have some pity, Ernest, you were once a newbie."

"Ha, I never got lost a day in my life."

"I never got lost a day in my *nine* lives."

Faint chuckling faded into nothingness.

Peg woke with a start, surprised to see sun shining through the shades. Nipper sat staring at the window. His head turned toward Peg then back to the window. He barked.

She placed her feet on the floor on top of the covers that were strewn about on the side of the bed. Groggily, she rubbed her temples with her fingers. "What time is it?" She spoke over the dog's incessant noise and looked at the clock. "Oh my, we slept through the night." She surveyed the room. Nipper's barking intensified.

She stood up. "All right, I'm coming, I'm coming." The vague recollection of the weird visitors from last night crept around her foggy brain. Her skin crawled.

Such a creepy dream. Must have been the sun… made me delirious. They seemed so real… Oh my God, I need to get a grip. I have an overactive imagination.

The dog stopped his clamoring when he saw her approach. He sat up on his back feet, kangaroo mode, and pawed at something on the sill.

"Nipper, what is it? Another lizard. You're going to have to get used to them. We both are." He leapt backward then, regaining his courage, he crawled toward it, only to jump again once he got close.

Hmmm…
Looks strange…
Kind of…
Like a…
HAIRBALL.

Voice Message from Peg to Clark

"Hi! I can't wait for you to come home. Call me when you get this. The phone didn't ring when you called me and left a message. I don't know why it did that. It was sitting right next to me. When I tried to listen to your voicemail, I couldn't understand what you said… the connection was bad. Maybe it's because there are too many bridges around here. I don't know. That's probably not a thing. Well, I really want to talk to you. Please, please try again soon. Love you."

Text message from Peg to Clark

Hello? Maybe you can't access voice message.

Email from Peg to Clark

Just in case you can't get voice messages or
text messages, I want to tell you how much
I miss you and want you to come home. I had
the weirdest dream last night. I might be
going crazy – only kidding (but not really).
Also, I wish you had gotten around to paint-
ing the front porch. I went to Mass the
other day. Did you know that they pray for
hurricane safety during Mass? I'm thinking
that we should keep a pulse on the hurricane activity this year. I'll probably buy
some extra batteries. And maybe a seven-day
supply of non-perishable food, hand-operated
can opener, five gallons of drinking water
and (the guide says) plastic plates…
When does the *together* part start in Key
West? OXOXOXOX

Email from Clark to Peg

Peg,
I hope that you get this. It is impossible
to communicate out of Cuba. That is why they
need me so much here – to establish modern
communication with the world. The negotia-

tions are getting started and it looks like
I'll be here for at least another month or
so. I know this isn't what we planned, but
think of it for the greater good! I'd say you
could come here too, but the accommodations
are very rough (no air conditioning or toilet paper) and I'm working all of the time.
I'll email you as often as I can. Thank you
for being such a good sport (like you always
are).
My love to Nipper and you.
Clark

Email from Peg to Clark

I'm thinking that NO TOILET PAPER is a
strange reason for me not to come and see
you. AND if Havana is so close - WHY DON'T
YOU COME HOME? Totally NOT understanding
this situation… AND had we not already spent
ALL of our budgeted money to BUY A HOUSE
(your idea), I'd be outta here (no idea how
since I can't drive across a bridge and Nipper can't fly, but I'd figure it out). Either
you get your ASS home so we can discuss this
NEW development in our living situation, OR
ELSE!!!

Peg slammed the computer shut and marched to the kitchen
counter to rip the coconut man calendar to shreds. Shaking with
anger, she stomped around the room.

"Or else what, sweetie?" The voice came from nowhere. The
room fogged.

Peg stopped in her tantrum tracks. "Who said that? Who's there?" Her frizzy hair stood on end. Electricity in the house shut down, generating an eerie quiet.

"I told you, madam, you're being duped."

"You can't say that we didn't warn her," purred a second voice.

Peg crouched low and whispered, "Where are you? Nipper, come here." The dog cocked his head sideways in perfect sphinx-like form.

A booming voice resounded. "Madam, it's time for the kidney punch."

And just like that, the lights resumed power, the oven blinked the wrong time and the air conditioning cranked its way back to a tired hum.

Peg grabbed the garlic from the fridge and swung it around. "I don't need your help. Go away."

Silence.

Her sweaty palms activated the garlic cloves. The dog's nose followed Peg as she clomped through every room.

When there was no answer from her ethereal roommates, she went to the back door to continue the protection outside. Prepared for a fight with the stubborn door, she was thrown backward when, to her surprise, the door opened without argument.

The sky was a brilliant blue. White puffy clouds, cartoonish in their perfection, floated by. The sun gleamed through the palm trees that swayed in the breeze. A blast of air carried some rare coolness from the Gulf of Mexico.

Peg took it in.

This is silly, I'm overwrought and hearing things.

She collapsed in a chair. Her lip quivered. "Oh, Nipper, my friend. What am I going to do about all of this?"

Nipper found a sunny spot next to her on the deck and stretched out with a sigh.

Hot Again

"So, tell me why you couldn't stay in Chicago if he was gonna be gone anyway?" Trudy's cheeks flushed red as she interrogated the PC screen.

"I don't know... I don't get it. If only I could talk to him... straighten this out..." Peg's voice trailed off.

"No. Tell him you're leaving. Tell him this was not part of the deal–" She stopped short. "Let me see your face."

"No." Peg angled the PC camera at the sleeping dog.

"I want to see if you've been crying. Let me see your face."

"No, I'm fine. I'm trying to understand. He's setting up communications for a country that has been out of touch for half a century. This was unexpected."

"No shit. Everything seems conveniently unexpected."

"Trudy, it's simply a business trip." Peg trembled when she remembered the recent similar ghostly interrogation.

"I'm coming there. I can't get away right now. But I'm coming. In a few weeks. Doesn't sound like he'll be back by then, which suits me fine." Mid-sentence, Trudy pushed her glasses down below her nose, resting them on her upper lip. As she talked, the glasses bobbed and steamed with hot nostril fog. "*I'm* not abandoning you."

"*He's* not abandoning me... and it's really hot here and I know how you hate the humidity – but I would *love* to see you." Peg turned the PC upward for a brief drive-by close-up of a face that had most definitely been crying. Tears gurgled to the surface. Not wanting Trudy to see the blubbering, Peg turned sideways to look out of the window. "Oops – the yard guy is here. I need to talk to him."

"You don't have a yard guy."

"I didn't say *my* yard guy, I said *the* yard guy."

"I can tell that you've been crying. Let me see you."

Peg faced the camera again. "I'm trying not to cry, honestly.

But when you yell at me it makes me miss you even more. You really do know me." Before Trudy could respond she added, "*The* yard guy is the one who saved Nipper's life from the Bufo Toad. The iguanas are hanging out in the sapodilla tree in the backyard – pooping on everything. He said he could help if I needed it... like an iguana hit-man."

"I don't even know what you are talking about. Iguanas? Sapodillas? Are you living on planet Earth?"

"I know, right?" Peg's mood improved with the change of topic. "These iguanas are something out of *Jurassic Park* – the size of dinosaurs. Their poop is a combination of all the disgustingness in the universe, splattering in every texture, color and vile scent imaginable."

"My God."

"In general, I'm against killing, but I'm seriously reconsidering my philosophy when it comes to them. They eat the sapodilla fruit which is made of chickle... you know... like chicklets – the gum? Try getting that out of your hair."

"Did I just say that I was coming to visit you? Changed my mind."

Peg smiled. "Only kidding about it getting in my hair. Although, my hair couldn't look much worse than it already does."

Trudy added, "Iguana shit shampoo. I'll get the trademark. We'll be rich. By the way, what does *not-your-yard-guy* look like?"

"Pierre? He's very muscly and very tan. Why are you asking me that?"

"French? Très romantique. Just curious."

"Canadian actually. Curious, huh? I know you better than that."

"I'm thinking maybe he could be a big masculine shoulder you could lean on – in times of drought. Just sayin'."

"Hush. I mean it. Stop talking right now." Peg shook her head and pointed a finger at the screen.

"At least *Pierre* is *there*. Hey – rhymes too."

"Closing my computer now. Can't hear you. Go research tickets before you really change your mind about coming. Bye."

"I want a full report after you see—" Snap. Trudy's voice cut off under the PC cover.

Peg saw Pierre's truck across the street and felt the blood pool in her face and neck, making her ears hot.

What the heck? Why am I blushing? That is crazy. He's just a nice man who helped me. Stop blushing… not kidding. I'm pretty sure that's a sin. At least a lower category one… CATEGORY ONE? Stop thinking about hurricanes… grotto was old… not my fault.

Willing herself out of her own head, she turned to the sleeping dog. "Nipper, we haven't walked yet today. Wanna go?" She picked up his leash and shook it, attempting to rouse him. Nipper lifted his head when he heard the leash clinking. He eyeballed the moisture dripping down the glass door, calculated the outside air was 98 percent liquid then plunked his head back on the couch.

"Really, Nipper, just because we missed our tiny window of coolness today and the 'feels like' index has risen to 106, it doesn't mean we can lie around all day and watch movies, drink wine and eat chips." Peg stared at the immobile animal, then her shoulders slumped. "Or does it?" She tossed the leash to the ground, hit the power button on the remote, and sat down next to him. When his soft brown head nestled in her lap, he heaved a big sigh.

"Okay, you win." The weight of the dog's head and his complete napping contentment kept Peg from the Beringer and Doritos. Talking herself into it NOT being five o'clock anywhere, she surfed through the channels.

Gilligan's Island (NO)
Click
Cubs' home game at Wrigley Field (heavy sigh)
Click
Reality TV Cheating Husb—
Click
TV OFF

Peg leaned her neck over the back of the couch, mesmerized by the blades of the ceiling fan as they twirled. She closed her eyes to hear the droning of the rusty air-conditioning unit as it labored valiantly, taking on the whole of high-noon heat with a mere 115 volts.

I am so homesick. I miss my old life… STOP.

With no warning, Nipper sprang off of Peg's stomach, leaping from the couch and onto the floor. Hackles up, barking frantically, he bolted toward the door.

"Ugh, wow." Peg's eyes opened wide. Suspicious of *imaginary* haint houseguests, she stood up and surveyed the room.

Seeing nothing but a manic dog, she located the leash. "All right. All right. Hold still. Good grief. There – gotcha."

She tripped into her flip-flops as the dog pulled her outside to the sweltering hotness. In the mad rush to leave the house, she realized she had forgotten to put on her hat. Her hair curled to a layer of protective frizz, but that was no match for the sun's rays lasering through to the skin on her head like she was a plucked chicken.

The dog continued his crazed behavior. "Nipper, what in the world is wrong with you? Is it a killer frog?" He dragged her close to a large shrub on the outside of the fence. He army-crawled, pawed at the bush, then kangaroo-hopped backward.

"Nipper, really. All this fuss for some old junk left by the… hey what's this?" Peg leaned down to see two mismatched shoes sticking out of the bottom of the bush. She removed the branches to reveal feet, attached to legs, attached to a body – which wasn't moving.

Peg jerked up. "Ahhh… someone HELP." The dog froze, fixated and on-point, his bird-dog instincts indicating that this was an excellent find.

"What eez it?" Pierre ran to them from the neighbor's backyard, the knight in shining, sinewy armor, glistening as he approached.

"A person's feet… and body too… not moving… looks dead. Do you have a phone? We should call 911. Or I'll go and get mine in the house." Peg covered the sides of her face with her hands.

"Let me see." Pierre knelt on one knee. When he separated the greenery, a human form appeared along with a horrendous stench.

"Oouf." Pierre stood up and waved the smell away with his

hand. "Eet eez a man." He pushed Nipper back who was sniffing the area in big sharp inhales.

"Is he alive? Doesn't smell like it. This is horrible." Peg pinched her nose with thumb and forefinger while also trying to keep ahold of the insanely curious dog.

Pierre kicked at the mismatched shoes with his own large work boot. Nothing. He kicked again. Nothing. With the third kick, the branches moaned and cursed. The shoes moved.

"I have seen zees before. I'll get eem out of zere." He put on his work gloves and leaned over the body while holding his breath. Pierre clutched the man's ankles and dragged him out from under the landscaping.

The man's shoes fell off revealing filthy feet with long, moldy nails curled over blackened toes. Coughing and wheezing, covered in dirt, he emerged to the sound of glass bottles clinking around him. He lay face up, bearded and toothless with pock-marked skin showing through his grimy tattoos. His pants were unzipped.

Peg turned her face to gag, then coughed away the urge. "He's alive, at least mostly alive, I think. Should I call an ambulance? Or the police? Nipper, get away." She caught the dog as he lifted his leg to relieve himself over the most enticing of all fragrances – eau de bum. "Nipper, no." The dog complied, lowering his leg halfway, but keeping it on the ready, just in case there was another window of opportunity.

"Are you okay?" Peg breathed through her mouth as she spoke. The man rolled to one side, then onto all fours. The back of his pants were dark and suspiciously stained, creating olfactory over-load for the salivating dog. The stinky street person stood up. Weebling one way and wobbling the other, his exposed bare butt cheek confirmed speculation about the chemistry of the stain. Peg gagged for real this time.

"Hell no. Leave m'alone," the man growled. "Git yur damn dog away from me." Nipper sidled his way next to the man and was balancing on three legs.

"Oh, I'm so sorry. Nipper, no." Peg pulled the dog and he reluctantly resumed his four-legged stance.

"You can't stay ere meester. Eets trespassing."

The man bobbed and weaved while steadying himself back into his mismatched shoes. "I kin stay wherever I want," he mumbled under his bad breath, then stumbled away from the group. His pants barely kept a PG-13 rating as he held them up with one hand.

"Hey, what about your garbage too, meester?" Pierre pointed to several empty liquor bottles, beer cans and cigarette packs.

Ignoring Pierre, the man zigzagged across the street.

"Zere is a homeless shelter in town," Pierre yelled into the vagrant's back.

The man turned and shouted back in a raspy, gravelly voice, "I ain't goin' there – won't let me drink. Treat me like a baby. I'm an a-dult... old enuff to drink. Can't make me shower... bastards." His shout fell to a mutter as he shuffled away with his Nike and Florsheim alternately shushing and clopping.

"Will he be okay?"

Pierre shrugged. "Zis eez a big problem. I try to elp as much as I can."

The dog continued to strain against the leash, his canine nose moist and flared in an attempt to catch every last molecule of the delectable shrub-squatter stench.

"Every day I go to the beach and see eef any of zem want to work." Pierre glanced over at Charles who had started to clean up the garbage from under the bush. "Charles eez different. Ee wanted to change. Most of zem don't. Zey want to drink." Pierre handed Charles a Hefty bag.

Those are very blue eyes. He's a nice man... with strong, rippling muscles. What are you doing? The heat is getting to me. Stop looking! He's probably married. What are you talking about? You are married. You have a husband with muscles. I miss my husband with muscles. I would like to touch those muscles. Oh, I'm so hot... but not in a good way.

Peg's reverie was prematurely terminated by a new commotion.

"Nipper Zee Dog – eez running away." Pierre took off after the dog who had backed out of his collar and made a beeline for the corner of the street.

"Nipper, come here," Peg yelled, frantically flip-flopping behind Pierre's work boots. "Why are you acting all crazy?" She stopped to catch her breath when she saw Randolph turn the corner holding Lulu on his hip. Nipper sat at his side, licking the little dog's dangling feet.

Pierre got there first and held the vizsla around the shoulders until Peg could fasten the now-tightened collar on the dog's neck.

"Ello, Randolph. Ello, Lulu."

Peg was shocked to see the chihuahua accept a friendly behind-the-ear scratch from Pierre.

"So you guys know each other?" Peg wheezed, making a mental note that she should get more exercise.

"Yes, of course. Good to see you, Pierre," Randolph replied.

"You too." Pierre wiped the sweat from his brow with his shirt sleeve.

Randolph added, "I see there is true animal magnetism going on here."

Peg blurted, "Well, I mean my husband *is* coming back soon… or pretty soon… I think… so crazy… Cuba and technology… and…"

Randolph gave her a sideways glance. "I meant with the *dogs*."

"Oh, yes. Yes. Of course. What else would you… of course…" Peg stammered.

"So, how *do* you two know each other?" Randolph made a kissy face at Lulu who lifted her top lip and bared her teeth.

"I… um… There was just a bum. I thought he was dead. Pierre has saved me many times… well… not many… But for sure a couple… I mean… we've always been *outside of the house*… because… where else would we be? But you are always welcome to come *in* the house… both of you… whenever you want… 'cause it's hot out here. Right?" Peg fanned herself with her hand.

"I work for zee neighbor next door," Pierre said, unflustered.

Randolph's eyes squinted in Peg's direction.

"How do *you* know Pierre?" Peg hoped her open-ended question would give her a reprieve from:

EVER TALKING AGAIN.

"Pierre is quite famous on the island actually. He is an excellent fisherman and has won lots of tournaments. Didn't you win with that 800-pound swordfish last year? I would sell my soul for that boat of yours. She's a real beauty," Randolph gushed.

Pierre flashed a huge boyish grin. "Yes, she's a good boat. I have three new four-fifty Yamahas for her zees year. So fast."

"Oh my. I'd love to have that wind beneath my wings," Randolph tittered.

Hmmm… now who's attracted to whom?

"Lobster mini-season eez soon. Eets my favoreet time of year."

"What's lobster mini-season?" Peg asked, already forgetting her vow of silence.

"Eets only for two days, but I love to have zee freedom to catch zee lobsters before zee commercial fishermen do. Eets magical. Zey taste so delicious."

Randolph nodded in agreement. "I absolutely love, love, love mini-season. I can grill a mean lobster. Hate to brag, but it's true."

Pierre beamed. "Why don't you come as my guests? Both of you. We can spend zee day catching lobsters and you can cook zem for us." He grabbed both Randolph and Peg's forearms as he spoke. Peg felt a zing. She thought she saw Randolph swoon.

"Shut the front door. This cannot be true. An invitation to go out on the ocean with you, a Key West icon, and in that boat, the most gorgeous girl on the sea? During mini-season? Shut UP." Randolph spun around, waving his arms and stomping his feet. Lulu started to bark. "Count me IN."

"Zat is great. Peg, what about you?"

Peg felt queasy under Pierre's azure gaze. Before she could say no, Randolph added, "Peg's in too."

"Oh… I don't know. Honestly, I'm not that good at ocean stuff." She big-eyed Randolph. "I don't know what I'm doing and I don't want to be a problem."

"Zere will be no problem. Eet eez easy and you will love eet."

"We'll have bottled water on the boat and lots of sunscreen, honey. It's a Key West must-do." Randolph put Lulu on the ground so that she could lovefest with Nipper.

Nipper and Lulu found a shady spot and settled down facing each other. The big dog's tongue drooped out of the side of his mouth as the small dog licked the drool drops before they hit the sidewalk.

Randolph seems really excited about this. He must want me to go for some reason. He's the one who volunteered me. I do owe him. It's not like I have to check my busy schedule.

"Oh, why not?" Peg assumed a casual manner as her armpit sweat and muffin top sweat hula-hooped around her waist.

"Zat is great. I will let you know when we will go. I haf to go now. Charles eez waiting." Pierre's carved calves about-faced and led him down the street.

Peg looked over at the truck in the hope of thanking Charles, but he was nowhere to be seen. She waved in the general direction anyway.

Peg turned to Randolph and said, "Why did you insist that I come too? You know what an ocean wreck I am. You have experienced that first hand."

"Listen, doll, this is a once-in-a-lifetime experience. Pierre invited *both* of us to go," Randolph said as he pointed at Peg and then back to himself. "And *I* want to go. It was a package deal and *you* are part of the package – like it or not. Lobster mini-season is only once a year. It is like a national holiday. And, the chance to go with Pierre? On his boat? Sister, I have dreamed of that. This is bigger than front-row tickets to Cher, or Barbra Streisand, or Bette Midler or – ALL THREE."

Taking a step back from his dramatic gesticulations, Peg held up her hands in defense. "Okay. Okay. Fine. I said I'll go. I just don't want any surprises. I'd really like to know what's in store for me so that I can be prepared. When is this *holy* day?"

Randolph pursed his lips. "It just so happens I have that information." He cleared his throat, newscaster-like. "The two-day spiny lobster sport season is always the last consecutive Wednesday and

Thursday in July. It begins at one minute past midnight on the last Wednesday in July and ends at midnight on the last Thursday in July."

Peg laughed. "Exactly 47 hours and 59 minutes. That is very precise. Who has the job policing this? Lobster cops? What if you start a minute earlier?"

"Not funny, Peg. It is a punishable offense. The rules are very specific. I don't want to have to fish you out of the pokey for not following the Florida Fish and Wildlife Commission laws. It's a federal crime." Randolph's voice was stern.

Peg giggled, then realized he was being serious. She covered her mouth and nodded her head. "Right."

"Only last week a guy was sentenced to prison for catching an undersized, pinched, out-of-season spiny lobster."

"Prison? I'm all for conservation but it's kind of like catching a fish, right? Not like drug running or armed robbery for heaven's sake." Peg could not suppress the grin this time.

Randolph gasped. "Every fish has its own season. It's not a joke. My husband is on the FWC and, believe you me, this is no laughing matter. He carries a gun." His shoulders shook as he quivered. "The stories he tells about the abuse of the sea creatures. Horrific." He placed his hands on his hips.

"Oh. You're married?" Peg asked, grateful to change the subject and also curious. "What's your hus– What's his name?"

He nodded. "One of the first gay couples to get hitched on the island. Bernie and I have been together for 18 years. It was a joyous occasion."

"I'm glad for you. Well, I mean I'm not GLAAD… of course I support GLAAD… but I'm not a lesbian… obviously 'cause I'm married to a man… I mean he's not here… but he's coming back. I mean I'm happy for you. I've never known…"

"Thanks, honey." Randolph saved her from drowning in awkwardness. "Bernie travels a lot with his job. I'm the stay-at-home dad." He pointed to Lulu, who, in perfect teenage-girl form, ignored him completely.

"I guess you could say that I'm a stay-at-home mom now too."

She thought of Clark and felt the sad pit in the middle of her stomach. "I don't know what I'd do without Nipper." Peg crouched down to pet the dog. He blinked his dreamy eyes and licked the salty perspiration off her hand. Her heart melted. "I'm still not sure about this lobster hunting, but it seems like I'm going. I'll do some research so that I'm not altogether clueless."

"It's called lobster mini-season and it's next week. And yes, *you are* going. Put your number in my phone so I can text you with the details." Randolph handed the phone to Peg.

She took off her sunglasses, held the phone at different angles, and squinted, but the sun's reflection made it impossible for her to see anything on the smudgy screen. Noticing that Randolph was giving her a "you can't even do this simple task" look, she said, "My fingers are too slippery. I have your number. I'll text you." Peg handed the phone back.

"Okay. Don't forget." Randolph picked up Lulu. "Too hot to be a bitch?" He kissed her on the nose as they walked away. The little dog hung limp in his hand, uttering only the most imperceptible of growls.

"See ya." Peg shaded her head from the sun. "Ugh. I'm fried. Let's go Nip. That's enough excitement for one afternoon."

The dog slowly got to his feet. His tongue made a clicking noise as it motored up and down.

"The good news is that it is definitely five o'clock somewhere."

Important Research

Beep. Beep. Beep.

Beep. Beep. Beep.

Peg sprung upright in her bed. Rays of sunlight made a checkerboard pattern on the rumpled covers over the sleeping dog.

Noon? What?

Text from Trudy

Why aren't u answering my chat request?

Frazzled and disoriented, Peg plopped her feet on the floor and found her phone on the dresser. The mirror reflected a mountain of disheveled hair that went to sleep damp and woke up the same way.

At least I showered. It had been a couple of days... or maybe more...

She observed her orange fingertips as she swept the Cheetos crumbs off of the sheets.

Next time I'll shower after the midnight snack. Thank God Trudy can't see me. She's probably already accomplished a million things today.

Text back to Trudy

Internet is out. Don't know why. Repair guy coming later.

Text to Peg

What about ur phone? What r u doing now?

Text to Trudy

Phone is buggy too. Signal here is weak. Getting ready to go to library to use internet. Researching lobster catching. Regular day in Key West. Ha ha.

Peg dragged herself to the bathroom.

Ha ha... more like ho-hum.

After staring at her toothbrush for 73 seconds, she brushed her teeth through cheesy lips while her hair flopped into the spit as she rinsed. Gathering the minty hair strands, she tied them into a scrunchy knot at the top of her head.

Text to Peg

Gonna get my ticket today. You heard from Clark?

Text to Trudy

YAY and NO : (I'll call u later.

```
Text to Peg

A-hole
```

She hadn't told Trudy, or anybody else for that matter, about the visits from the haints. She didn't want Trudy to have additional ammunition against Clark, even if it was provided by the undead. Also – she wanted to avoid getting thrown into the local insane asylum.

She thought about how her life had changed in the last few months. She had been a valued partner in the marriage before. This wasn't a part of the drunken-napkin agreement.

Bouncing up and down to physically shake off the emotion, Peg shoved the phone in her bag then removed it a second later.

I forgot to text Randolph. He'll be freaking out by now.

She texted while walking to the treat cupboard to remove the bag of pig ears. Hearing the crinkle sound of the plastic, the thrilled dog leapt in the air, tail wagging furiously.

"I'm going out for a while, Nipper. Okay, calm down. Sit." The dog quieted and sat at attention. "Good boy. Here you go." She held out the flattened triangular remnant of pig, the coarse hair petrified to the sticky dead skin.

"These are disgusting."

The dog disagreed. He trotted across the room with the crusty carcass in his mouth. Placing it down, he licked it smooth and slimy.

"That should keep you occupied."

Peg stepped out of the house with her sunglasses in her right hand. She took one step then hesitated, looked down at her glasses, waited a minute until full fog had taken effect, then used her not-yet-soaking-wet tee shirt and wiped off the lenses. Holding her head high, she saw the world clearly.

Learning curve kicking in.

Fifteen seconds later, complete blindness. She cleaned them off again, this time with the now-sweaty shirt.

My God. Even the humidity is humid.

She longed to get in her car and crank the air conditioning, but didn't want to unpark only to get into a street fight for accessible library parking with future "Silver Alerts" in their Impala sedans. She walked by her dusty car on the street and noticed it had a flat tire.

Ugh... such a sad neglected car... you miss your garage, poor thing. Clark used to take care of you too.

The poinciana trees mushroomed flame-colored flowers above her head. Turbulent gray thunderheads threatened a summer squall from all directions. Peg figured out two umbrellas ago that the wind and the rain dumps were too powerful for even the hardiest of Midwestern-made protection. Keeping a plastic garbage bag in her backpack, she felt fully prepared for any sudden storm.

Walking along White Street, she saw the line forming at Sandy's Cafe, the local Cuban establishment famous for their Cuban coffee and sandwiches.

I could use a cup of coffee.

Peg ambled over to the disorganized crowd at the front walk-up window. Tourists spoke in many different languages, English not being one of them. She noticed the line was significantly smaller next to the tiny unobtrusive window at the other side of the cafe – the one inside the laundromat.

This is actually a genius business plan... make laundry a social event and sell coffee and food.

She walked around the street corner and into the laundromat. The rows of washers and dryers were spinning while clusters of people chatted in small groups around the machines. Several young military personnel called out their con leche orders into the window, while the Sandy's staff handled an impossible amount of multitasking behind the scenes.

Peg tapped the shoulder of a tall female navy officer, who, based on the uniform decorations, looked like she was in charge. "Excuse me, Officer..." Peg read the name tag. "... Trindl, is it? Is this window reserved for military? Can civilians order here too?"

Officer Trindl's chin jutted out – the brim of her hat pulled low. Her piercing brown eyes deliberately descended to Peg's level. "You can call me Patty." She tilted her head forward. "This window is a best-kept secret – locals only."

Peg straightened her posture. "I'm Peg. I just moved here."

The officer drilled. "You a snowbird?"

Peg shook her head. "No... umm... full time. All the time. I can't... I mean... I don't leave."

With great authority the imposing officer motioned a hand sweep. "Step aside, sailors, this woman needs to place an order."

Peg marched up to the window.

If it's good enough for the United States Navy, then it's good enough for me.

"Con leche, please." She spoke with confidence, like she'd done this hundreds of times before.

"Con azucar?" the man behind the counter asked.

"Excuse me?" Peg shrank.

Ugh, not again.

Officer Trindl rescued her. "He wants to know if you want sugar in your coffee. I highly recommend it for plebes."

"Oh, yes please, con azucar then." Peg mouthed *thank you* to her rescuer.

She gave Peg a thumbs up with one hand as she sipped the hot liquid in the styrofoam cup with the other.

Waiting for her coffee, Peg couldn't help but overhear the conversation of a couple of teenagers in the laundromat. They were saying things like – *debit and credit.* It made her spreadsheet senses tingle.

Ahhh, words I understand.

The teens leaned over their finance books with yellow markers in hand.

"So is a debit like a debit card?" The teen's tattooed hand scratched his shaved head.

"I don' know, bro, and is a credit like a credit card?" The friend twirled his eyebrow ring and leaned back in exasperation.

"We're not gonna pass this final, bro. This sucks."

Peg moved in closer. "Hello, gentlemen. I'm sorry to eavesdrop, but maybe I can help. Can I see the question in your school book?"

The first teen said, "Sure, lady." He handed Peg the book.

Peg studied the page. "Okay, so all of your asset accounts will be debit balances, while all of your liabilities will be credit balances. There are exceptions of course, but I won't get into them here."

Blank stares.

"Okay. Let's look at it this way, think of debit and credit as yin and yang. For every debit there must be an equal credit amount. For example, when you take a hundred-dollar loan, you record the hundred dollars to debit – right? But what else would happen?" Peg pointed to the numbers on the page.

"You keep the cash and run?" The boys elbowed each other and chuckled.

"If you want to go to prison, sure. But if you are an upstanding fiduciary, you record that hundred dollars as a credit balance to Note Payable in your Liabilities."

"Like an IOU?"

"Exactly. Well done." Peg handed the book back. The boys smiled.

A voice called out from behind the counter, "Con leche for Peg."

"Oh, that's me." Peg waved in the direction of the window. "I'm headed to the library now." She took out a pen and yanked a napkin out of the holder. "Anyway, here's my cell phone number. Feel free to text me if you have any other questions about the material. My name is Peg Savage, by the way. I'm from... well... I live down the street."

"Uhh. Thanks Peg, I'm Tom and this is my buddy Steven. We gotta pass this class."

She shook both of their hands and handed Tom the napkin. "You can do it. Finance is fun once you get the hang of it."

Peg gave the teens a thumbs up with one hand as she sipped the hot liquid in the styrofoam cup with the other.

Continuing on her way, Peg circumvented a family of Asian tourists who blocked the sidewalk while taking pictures of the chickens that gathered by the side of the road. The dappled rooster crowed and put on a show. Two rowdy toddlers chased a pack of peeping baby chicks under a bench while both species of mothers clucked corrections to their offspring.

Approaching the stucco library building, Peg recognized the Florsheim and the Nike next to the bike rack. Abandoned by the shrubbery squatter, the shoes sat empty, without their original partners – without a job to do – forsaken. Peg felt a sudden somber kinship for these faithful, hardworking shoes, so callously cast aside. A giant, mildewy, stuffed ostrich occupied the back seat of a tandem bike. The big bird's feet were duct-taped to the pedals, forcing its long legs to splay awkwardly. The front bike seat sat empty – only a beer can in a coconut cup holder as proof of a prior resident. The double-seated bike leaned precariously against a towering banyan tree, whose roots hung down over the ostrich in long tendrils, giving the wide-eyed bird a surprised inmate look.

Peg stared at the imprisoned ostrich.

I'd like to set you free… then you'd be Free Bird…

"If I leave here tomorrow…" she hummed.

Oh… bad song… stopping now…

The musty coolness of the concrete building goose-pimpled her skin. The worn, green floor tiles echoed as she stepped. The air smelled of disinfectant and vestiges of whatever the disinfectant failed to disinfect. The yellow fluorescent lights dimmed as the island sucked electricity from mainland Florida. A man with a pony-sized Rottweiler waited in line at the information desk. In front of him, a woman holding a toddler on her hip chatted with the librarian. The dog panted and drooled, while pressing its nose into the baby's diapered butt as it dangled in front of him.

The child squealed in delight at this game while the unconcerned mother continued her conversation. The toddler squirmed in her arms until he was put down onto the floor – to *play* noisily with the 200-pound dog.

Not exactly the Chicago Public Library.

Peg found the Wi-Fi code listed on a poster hanging next to a desk with a snoring library patron; head back, throat exposed, his pungent breath filling the air. Finding a small table in the corner that had goodish ventilation, she sat down, picked up the bottom of her shirt and wiped the sweat from her face, not caring who might see her exposed fleshy belly – something she would never have thought of doing in her past life – just months ago. Energized with having a project to distract her, she began her studying.

This time I'm going to be PREPARED.

She logged into Google and typed in: "How to catch a Florida lobster."

A Florida lobster travels forward by walking slowly. When they are scared they flip their tail and propel backward. They have no claws.

Like this is gonna be hard to do? They are slow, backward-moving, with no defense.

Locate a lobster under a rock or in a hole.

The water is clear with good visibility. Check.

Use tickle stick and slide it behind the lobster. Gently tap on its tail. If it doesn't walk forward be more aggressive.

Aggressive with a tickle stick – sounds almost humane.

Place net behind the lobster and trap it between ground and net. If it doesn't respond, tap it on the forehead.

I've had college roommates wake me up the same way. It works.

Swoop net around so lobster is trapped. Close the net.

Easy. Peasy.

Must measure the lobster's body, needs to be at least three inches from eyes to end of carapace.

Carapace? Sounds like an Italian pasta.

No pregnant lobsters.

Gross.

Can only catch six lobsters per person per day.

How about how many per MINUTE? Because I'll be so AMAZ-ING.

Peg rolled her shoulders and closed her eyes for a moment's meditation. Her jaw muscles relaxed as she mentally visualized her success. Formulating plans followed by researched execution of project goals – this was her wheelhouse. She predicted her future success with positive imagery.

I will rock at catching lobsters.

When she opened her eyes, Peg noticed a skinny teenage girl staring at her. Behind that girl, stood a few boys and behind them, two more girls. The gang of teenagers hovered over the table.

"Can I help you?" Peg asked as they moved in closer.

"Are you Peg Savage?" The skinny girl spoke. "Tom texted me you'd be here." She took her finance book out of her backpack.

"Yes, I am. Ahh, okay. I recognize that book." Peg made eye contact with each student. "Do *all* of you need help?"

"We have to pass this summer school class or we can't graduate. So unfair," a boy with an '80s mohawk groused. "It's really hard and the teacher doesn't have time to tutor outside of the classroom. Some dumb excuse like she's teaching a bunch of other classes and she's got a million kids of her own." The others nodded their heads and grunted in solidarity. "Like she wants us to fail." He threw his backpack to the floor for effect.

"Well, it does sound like she's stretched in a lot of different directions." Peg stood up and looked around the room. "Okay, well, everyone grab a chair and let's see what we can do. Normally, I would think that it would bother the other patrons in the library to have a teaching session, but since there are no other patrons here, I think we're all right."

"I've never been in the library before. It's so old school," one girl said as she sat down.

A boy added, "I hadta pick up my dad from here once. He borrowed a tape for his ancient VHS player. VHS – what a dinosaur."

Peg added, "Well, I thought the Beta recorder was the way to go. Who knew VHS would be so popular?" When no one joined in with an opinion, she continued, "Enough high-tech talk. Do you all have the same study guide as Tom?"

All nodded.

"Please take it out and we'll start there."

"I really hate this subject," the skinny girl whined as she removed the stapled papers from her notebook.

Peg held up a pointer finger. "Just so you know, workers in the finance industry have the lowest incidence of fatality in the workplace. We're *safe* and *sound*." When she saw the eyes roll she added, "I mean it's something to think about. World's deadliest catch or cushy office?"

The teen mumbled, "I'd rather risk my life as a bullet tester."

"Right… okay… moving on… So, who has questions?"

The hands went up.

After the last finance book and backpack departed, the library was quiet aside from the occasional snort and phlegm cough emanating from behind the bookshelves. Peg rose from her chair with a sense of accomplishment and gathered her belongings.

She glanced over to the counter displaying newspapers. A Spanish headline caught her eye in the *Tribuna de la Habana*.

Havana… as in Cuba…

A large picture took up most of the front page. In it, a collection of people crowded next to each other. They linked arms and smiled as if someone in the gathering had just told a joke. The women were tanned and slim with long dark hair. The men were dark skinned, fit and–

Peg yanked the newspaper from the rack. Folding the paper to get a better look, she honed in on the image of the man at the edge of the group. His biceps bulged as he draped his arm across the shoulder of the insanely gorgeous woman next to him, her thick dark mane gathered to one side, cascading in rivulets down to her tiny waist. Their laughing mouths opened wide as the man and woman faced each other in what seemed like a private moment captured in a public venue. The man's toned legs pointed down to huarache sandals bought from Target (size 11).

Clark.

Peg stopped breathing. The newspaper's black ink smudged as her clammy hands soaked the words.

This is why he's too busy to talk to me? He looks busy all right.

The room spun.

Can't breathe. Gotta get out of here.

The moldy, stale air closed in on her. Without thinking, she jammed the newspaper in her backpack and moved in the direction of the exit, inadvertently stepping on a man curled up in the library foyer. Briefly staring at him without apology, she ignored his boisterous admonitions and continued out of the door.

Her brain froze in a protective zombie state as she autopiloted back to the house – right at the light, left at the corner, left into the gate.

Not noticing the pile of pig-ear throw-up next to the coffee table, she sat down on the couch. The dog jumped up next to her, confused by the lack of greeting. His anxious eyebrows flicked up and down as he nudged his head under her lifeless hand. Since the hand refused to pet him, he sat up and licked Peg squarely on the lips. The pig-ear vapors and sandpaper tongue broke her trance.

"Nipper." She hugged the dog.

Regaining use of her panic-stricken fingers, she picked up her phone, swiped and…

Nothing.

She held the newspaper close to her face.

He's touching her so casually… I know that touch… I know that look…

The tears dripped slowly at first, but soon rivers of black ink trailed across the soggy paper. Her heart squeezed so tight that she clutched her chest as the sobs choked out in loud gasps. She stood up and paced around the room, the concerned dog at her heels.

Gotta think… gotta get a grip.

Teeth gritted, she pounded her fists on the top of her head and rope-jumped her feet in full tantrum.

Hands covering her face, she cleared her lungs with a deep exhale. When she pulled her hands away, gooey strands of prior postnasal drip clung to her fingers, making a cat's cradle of snot.

"Yuck."

Clasping her hands back together, she big–stepped to the kitchen counter and plucked a tissue with such force the box flipped to the ground.

"Son of a…" She kicked the box and watched it sail in the air, across the wood floor, under the table, next to the couch and through the unattended pile of puke, making a chunky trail before it tumbled to a stop.

"Arrrrgh." She blew her red nose with a high-pitched squeak.

Get it together.

While she was assessing her pity-party damage, the doorbell rang. The dog vaulted over the back of the couch, barking with joyous excitement, practically knocking Peg over as she turned the knob to open the door.

Internet guy… I forgot.

Had Peg looked out of the window first before answering the door, she most certainly, positively, without question, would not have opened it. There stood before her the most colossal ruffian of a man.

"Ahh." Peg took a step back. "I mean, hello."

"Hello, ma'am, I'm with the cable company." The dog rose to his back feet and hugged the immense waist of the visitor. "Hi there, Nipper." The man leaned over and nuzzled the dog.

"How do you know–?" Peg stopped when she noticed the tell-tale Adam's apple tattoo – skull and crossbones – rising and falling. "Big Jim?"

"Yes, ma'am." He pointed to his name tag which said – James McPhearson ATT&T Technician.

"You're not doing the moving company stuff anymore? Nipper, get down." Peg reached for the dog.

"He's okay. Remember me, boy?" Nipper licked Big Jim's scruffy handlebar mustache. The dog hesitated for a second, chewed a bit of something then resumed his task. "Haha. He must have found a bit of lunch in there."

Peg winced.

"I still do the moving company. It's slow right now – summertime. I moonlight at this job – during the day." He laughed a big guffaw and the crossbones criss-crossed.

"Please come in – that is, if you can get around Nipper." Peg opened the door wide and the massive man tenderly placed the dog back on all fours and then lumbered past her into the narrow hallway.

"The cable box is at the end of the hall." Peg pointed and let the oversized technician lead the way. Big Jim barely fit between the walls.

"I just come from a restaurant down the street. Best part of this job is eating for free at the local establishments. Y'ever been to Nimfo's?" Big Jim asked over his shoulder as he sucked at his teeth.

"No, um, not yet. The name… I don't know," Peg stuttered. "I've had takeout from Fishy Delight though. That was good." Peg spoke to his broad backside.

Big Jim stopped short. Peg bonked into him like a flea into a rhino. He turned to face her, "Ma'am, I wouldn't go to Fishy's if I was you. I do the Internet installations at all of the restaurants – and, believe you me, I see all kindsa nasty stuff in some kitchens, and Fishy's? They're the worst. Rats. Cockroaches. Termites. No hand-washing, if you get my drift."

"Oh my God." Peg's stomach recoiled when she remembered the green stuff in Fishy's fish tacos. "How can they stay in business? What about the health inspector?"

"Money talks. Health inspector walks." Big Jim chuckled. "Ma'am, you all right? You look a bit under the weather. Where else you' been eatin'?"

"I'm fine. Thank you. Just a summer cold." Peg glanced at herself again in the mirror as she walked by. "Oh my, I *do* look horrible, kinda like rode hard and put up wet." She paused. "I mean if I was a horse… that was ridden hard… and well… put back in the stall without anyone taking care of it…" Her voice trailed off.

Big Jim patted her on the arm. His gargantuan calloused hand felt incongruously tender and soft on her skin. Peg let his hand rest there longer than she intended.

My God, I really am lonely… don't cry… don't cry…

Pivoting around to face the other direction, she opened up the nearest closet door. "It's kind of a small space."

"This is Key West. I've seen tighter squeezes." Big Jim winked a huge eye. "I'll have you up and running in no time."

Some 'Splainin' To Do

Peg held the newspaper to the phone to take a picture of Clark and the woman. She scrolled in so that the couple's laughing faces took up the entire screen.

Click
Copy
Contacts
Clark

Text message from Peg to Clark

?

SEND

Peg paused for a few minutes then decided to add:

Text message from Peg to Clark

```
Looks like you are too busy working to com-
municate with your WIFE.
```

SEND

Text message from Peg to Clark

```
I've noticed that you don't seem to have
any issues cashing checks in Cuba. Maybe it
would be easier for you to communicate with
me by writing notes on the bottom of the
```

> cashed checks. They come in faster than your
> emails.

SEND

Not ten minutes later, Peg heard the not-so-familiar ding of the phone notifying her of an email.

Email from Clark to Peg

I am so sorry that I haven't been able to
be in touch with you. Yes, the hotel has
been so accommodating and agreed to cash my
checks. I have been working long hours and it
is next to impossible to communicate inside
or outside of this country. The picture you
sent me was with my translator, Ita. I can
explain. It's not what it looks like. I know
this isn't what you were expecting when we
moved, but it won't be forever. The world is
changing and it is exciting to be a part of
it. You are doing your part too. I appreci-
ate your patience and support. I love you,
both you and Nipper! Give him a big kiss for
me. (Happy Face Emoji)
Clark

Peg read the email several times.

She folded up the newspaper photo and placed it in the drawer on top of the wilting drunken-napkin agreements.

Text from Peg to Clark

Get your ASS home.

Lobster Mini-Season Day

Happy to have the day planned out, Peg woke up early on lobster mini-season day. Randolph had texted the day before that he would pick her up at 6.30am.

The image of a shirtless, wet Pierre out on the open water kept popping up. She told herself not to think about *what if* Pierre DID like her in that way? What would she do?

Nothing... you would do nothing... you are being ridiculous...

The night before, after self-administering the hot-caramel-auburn hair coloring, she loofahed, exfoliated, shaved, shaved again, moisturized, moisturized again before she washed, rinsed, blew dry, straightened and then straightened again the hair that had not been out of a rubber band for months. Aware that any sudden head turning during sleep would encourage the hair to re-crinkle, she slept on her back, strategically placing her silky hair on the pillow, and willed her subconscious self to remain immobile. Every hour or so, she woke to check on the status, tamping and smoothing until she was satisfied with her hair's compliance.

That morning, there was a tiny bit of not-hotness in the air and she was relieved to discover that the lack of sun, on the 5.15am dog walk, allowed for minimal head and body sweat. She applied waterproof mascara, face foundation and a touch of lipstick. Opening the bottle of Clark's favorite perfume, she held it to her nose. She hesitated, then defiantly turned the bottle of perfume to her neck and pushed her finger on the squirter.

Never hurts to put your best foot forward.

Ahhh Ooooga. Ahhh Ooooga.

The dog popped his head up at the sound of the horn. She walked over to pet his cheek and he relaxed. "Nipper, you be a good boy. You've had your breakfast and a long walk, and done all of your business. You'll be fine for six hours." She talked more to herself than to the dozing dog who lay sprawled across the couch in centerfold fashion.

AHHH OOOOGA.

"Coming. Good grief." Peg grabbed her towel, beach bag, hat and purse and made sure that she had plenty of sunscreen. Double-checking herself in the mirror near the door, she adjusted the underwire of her slimsuit, wiggled everything into the proper place and scurried out the front door.

Randolph tossed his dive bag behind him to make room for Peg in the passenger seat of the Flintstones-mobile. "Come on, Doll. Let's go get some lobsters." He waved her in.

"Hi, Randolph. I'm ready." She showed him her large beach bag, "…and I froze the water bottles – thinking ahead." She pointed to her brain with her forefinger.

Randolph stared at her as she put on her hat. "I *see* that you *are* ready." He turned his body to face her. "Your hair looks very nice. I've never seen it straight before. A new color too?"

"Oh. Yes. Long overdue." Peg dismissed the attention.

"We're going on a boat, you know. A fast boat. It will mess up your hair." Randolph kept staring.

"I know that. Of course. Doesn't matter at all." Peg imagined the breeze blowing her silky auburn locks as Pierre admired her beauty. Hoping to change the subject she asked, "Where is Lulu today?"

"At home snuggled in her furs and diamonds. She'll be so bitter when I get back. Hates it when I leave her." Randolph pointed to Peg's beach bag. "Pierre will have a cooler of water on the boat, but always good to have more." He pressed his Sperry to the gas pedal and they putt-putted away. "I brought bottles of bubbly." He leaned toward her conspiratorially and elbowed her elbow. "What is a day on a fabulous boat without champagne?"

Peg relaxed. "I went to the library and did research on how to catch a lobster." She held on to her hat as a wind gust blew side-ways through the golf cart.

"The library? Who goes to the library?" Randolph slammed the brake to let the dregs of some late-night partiers cross the road. "The light is red, people," he yelled as they continued to pay no attention.

"My Internet was down–"

Randolph cut her off. "Sweetie, you are lucky you didn't catch something there. I mean, the bums have really taken it over."

Peg felt an imaginary something move in her scalp and scratched it.

"Bernie says I need to be more compassionate. Ha. Easy for him to say since he carries a G–U–N." He whispered the letters. "People don't mess with you when you have a G–U–N. So, people don't mess with him." He shook his head and laughed. "How did I get on this subject? I apologize. I'm so charged up today."

Peg smiled. "I learned about the tickle stick, and the net and measuring, and don't take the baby lobsters or pregnant lobsters."

"Right. Give a lobster mother a break. I mean really. When they are teenagers, she will be happy to have you catch them – or her for that matter. At least *my* mom would have." He tee-heed at his own joke and waved to a passing scooter.

Involuntarily following along, Peg raised her hand and waved.

Randolph chatted away. "Did you know that people are so friendly here that if you wave to one person it starts a chain reaction of waving? It goes all the way up the Keys until Miami. Then it stops. People don't wave in Miami." He tsk-tsked the Miamians.

Not knowing whether she should stop waving or not, Peg kept her hand held up in the Queen's wave, not above the crown, though, just to be safe. "Where's the boat? The same place as paddleboard yoga?" She winced at the memory.

"No. Pierre keeps it at the Key West Bight. He'll call ahead and they'll have the boat gassed up and ready for him. I can't wait for you to see this beauty," Randolph shouted as he drove.

Pierre is handsome... Wait... he's talking about the boat...

"Adventure time." As soon as the words came out of her mouth, she felt queasy.

Randolph maneuvered Betsy into a small space at the end of the crowded parking lot. People milled about, carrying coolers and nets. The captains yucked it up as their mates schlepped the provisions into the boats that lined up in formation as they waited to be boarded.

Gathering her belongings from the prehistoric golf cart, Peg saw Pierre at a distance. His strapping thighs bulged as he walked in their direction. Her salivary glands ceased and her legs jellied.

Really? What is wrong with you?

"This way, doll. Looks like his boat is first in line."

Struggling to keep up behind Randolph's big strides, Peg commanded her body to behave as they approached the boat.

"Ello. Good morning. Eet eez a beautiful day for catching lobsters." Pierre stood on the edge of the boat. His teeth were as white and gleaming as the boat itself.

"Hi, Pierre. Yes, this is going to be a wonderful day. Thank you so much for inviting me. Us." Randolph stood aside so that Peg came into view.

"Thank you," was all that Peg could squeak out from her dry mouth.

"Peg, let me elp you into zee boat." Pierre took Peg under the arm and guided her over the side. The build-up in her mind matching the electricity of his touch forced her to collapse onto the seat bench, still clutching her beach bag and towel. "Oh. Are you okay? Eet eez a bit wobbly." Peg thought she saw an aura of light around him.

"Thank you." Her tongue grew too large for its space.

That's all that you can say?

Randolph leapt in. "Peg, I'll put our stuff in the storage locker in back. You all right, sweetie? You look pale. You're not seasick already, are you?"

Peg woke out of her state. "No. I'm fine. Thank you." She handed over her beach bag and towel. "Can I help?" Her words were drowned out by the sound of the giant engines as they revved. She tried to stand but was off balance and flopped back down on the seat. She watched Pierre teach Randolph about the boat's equipment, overhearing words like "depth finder" and "outboard engine" over the din.

A woman approached the boat. Her long, thick, waist-length blonde hair moved naturally in rhythm with her tanned and toned legs. She sported a bikini top and cut-off shorts that were unzipped and folded over – a dazzling purple gem filling her belly button sparkled in the sun.

"Hi." The Barbie doll's voice was high-pitched and she gestured a rainbow-shaped wave.

Pierre looked up from the boat's controls and smiled a broad, handsome grin. "Ello, cherie." He walked over to her and, in one swift move, she vaulted over the side of the boat into his strong arms. "How are you, amour?" She nuzzled his neck and kissed him passionately on the lips.

Peg blushed.

Pierre placed her down, while keeping his hand on her young and sculpted buttocks. "Everyone, zis eez Lisa Nevins. She will be coming with us to catch lobsters. Lisa, zis eez Peg and Randolph." Pierre pointed to each of them.

"Nice to meet you, Lisa." Randolph yelled over the engine noise and shook her hand politely.

Peg made the tiniest attempt to move, then fell back, still unable to stand due to lack of balance and due to the new feeling of being socked in the gut.

What? He's got Miss Universe as a girlfriend? Actually... Miss TEENAGE Universe? Seeing that Peg was stuck in her seat, Lisa fluttered to the front of the boat and held out her slim, brown hand. Peg felt the cool, flawless fingers in her own greasy, clammy palm.

"Nice to meet you," Peg lied. "Sorry my *husband* couldn't be here too. I have a *husband* he's just not here right now. He's in Cuba... improving the world... making a difference. But he's coming back soon."

Peg avoided Randolph's stare.

"That's cool." Lisa's golden tresses left traces of lavender in the air as she moved about the boat.

"Shall we get going?" Pierre sat in the tall seat under the bimini. Lisa lifted the ropes from the dock then stood behind Pierre, hugging him with her lean arms, as he steered the boat away from the marina. Pierre smiled and waved at Peg as they gained speed past the channel markers.

Peg returned the smile and took off her hat and shook her hair in the wind, going for that "don't hate me because I'm beautiful" look. Unfortunately, her straight hair was at the perfect length to blow directly into her eyes, causing a sharp pain as each chemically treated strand whipped her corneas with knife-like precision. Turning her head to face the wind, her eyeballs watered, leaving a trail of crusty tears on her cheeks.

The ocean was crowded, from large yachts and fishing boats to kayaks and surfers with coolers. Pierre expertly piloted around all of them. The clear water reflected the colors of the sun rising through billowy clouds overhead. Peg took a minute from her troubles to admire the view.

"It's the most beautiful mixture of colors," she yelled over to Randolph as she held her hat back on her head.

"It's magical. It's why people come to the Keys," Randolph yelled back. "The water is warm and clear year round. Can't find that anywhere else in the US." His dimples strained from joyfulness.

After 15 minutes on the water, Pierre slowed the boat and studied the GPS. "I think zat zere will be good lobsters in zees area." When he cut the engines, he pushed a button and the anchor clanked its way down. Lisa watched over the front of the boat and gave him two perfect thumbs up when the anchor caught. Many other boats skulked around in close proximity. When they saw Pierre decide on the best location, they followed suit. It didn't take long for the boating neighbors to move in, turning open sea into open season.

Peg looked over the side of the boat. "It's pretty deep. We won't be able to catch any lobsters here," she said to Randolph, who was removing a mask and snorkel from a dive bag.

"What do you mean too deep? It's only eight or nine feet." He leaned over Peg's side of the boat to see what she was talking about. "It's clear. Hey, I see one. I'm going in. He's mine." Randolph pumped his fist. Pierre pumped his fist back.

Peg grabbed Randolph by the arm. "I mean, it's too deep to stand on the bottom and catch the lobsters... you know... tickle them… and scoop them up with a net… and be in the water while measuring them."

Randolph laughed and slowed his speech to preschool-teacher speed. "Peg, we are going to *swim* to the bottom – and catch them. With dive masks and snorkels. We use the nets and ticklers while *swimming* underwater."

"What? My research didn't say I had to *swim underwater* to catch them. I thought I would be wading in the water. It's not possible to do all of that upside down, underwater, *not breathing*. Are you listening?" Peg talked to an already geared-up Randolph as he jumped in the water, his flippers making a giant splash upon entry.

"It's fun." He swam on his back otter-style. "Watch me." He snorkeled to the side of the boat. "Hand me the tickler and gloves. This guy looks enormous."

Peg did as she was told and watched him hover in the water over his prey. As soon as he was in position, his butt went straight up followed by his flippers. He dove vertically to the crustacean and wedged the tickler behind his shell. When the lobster tried to make a getaway, Randolph trapped him in the net and brought him to the surface, holding the top of the net tightly.

He whooped and hollered, "First catch of the day." Randolph treaded water as he pried the catch out of the net and measured it with the other end of the tickler. "Meets the guidelines. People, we're eating well tonight." He tossed the lobster into the boat and it click-clacked around Peg's feet.

She jumped. "What are you doing? Doesn't it go in a bucket or something?"

"No time for buckets. We got hunting to do." Randolph put the snorkel in his mouth and swam in the other direction.

Before Peg could voice additional concerns about the creature crawling next to her, another lobster came flying over the side and landed at her feet. Lisa had slipped into the ocean like a mermaid, and, with no snorkel or fins, had caught the lobster with her bare hands. Pierre flashed his good-looking grin. "Peg, do you want to try eet? I have a mask and a snorkel and some feens eef you like."

Since doggy-paddling was not an option and remembering the

disastrous paddleboard yoga experience, Peg declined, saying, "I'm enjoying myself on the boat, just watching." She stifled a scream as another lobster whizzed past her, landing with a thud.

"Glad you can enjoy." Pierre dove into the water close to Lisa, who executed a porpoise dive under him. They frolicked and kissed as they rolled around each other.

My God, they can breathe under water. They are fish people.

Alone on the boat while the whoops of hunting success surrounded her, not to mention a growing number of very bummed lobsters, Peg journeyed to the cooler without stepping on anyone's dinner and opened the lid.

Champagne.

Towel in hand she scooped up the shiny bottle, covered up the top with the towel, and, using her well-trained champagne-opening thumbs, she popped the cork and poured herself a big plastic cup full of bubbles. Sitting on the bench among the scampering shellfish, she put her feet up – and drank. And drank. And drank. As each additional lobster hurtled by, she refilled her cup.

This isn't so bad… except for the impending doom of my creepy-crawly friends… they don't look that happy…

Randolph swam up. "Come on in, doll. You should try it."

Bolstered by the bubbly, she took off her cover-up, placed her feet wide for ballast and stood up to yank the bottom of her suit back down over the exposed parts. "I'll do it." She located a mask and snorkel. "I need something to hang on to. I'm not a great shwim… swimmer." The empty champagne bottle clinked across the boat.

Randolph's eyeballs rolled.

She pulled the rubber strap of the mask on her head, feeling her hair leave her scalp in hunks.

"Take the seat cushion. It floats," instructed Randolph.

"In case of a water landing, I get it." Peg giggled and threw the bright green seat cushion overboard, its fluorescent straps dangling spider-like in the water.

Cautiously sitting on the side of the boat, she plopped her body in. "Ooo. The water's so warm. Makes me have to pee." More gig-gling while she placed the floatation device under her.

Randolph moved away. "Stay *behind* me." He dove under water out to the open sea.

The sun's glare on the surface made it difficult to see anything. Peg decided not to follow Randolph and hung close to the boat. She saw Lisa and Pierre romping in the distance.

They probably have gills.

Gaining a bit of confidence, Peg ventured out and stuck her head in the water. One arm wrapped around the cushion allowed the other arm to paddle. After swallowing a considerable amount of salt water, she sort of got the hang of the snorkel and could breathe a few breaths without choking or burping.

Clark was right about the Keys... don't think about him. But he was right – this is something everyone should see...

Floating peacefully in a drunken dream, she observed the hidden world of ocean life. She laughed as a school of tiny striped fish darted around her. The coral blooms swayed with the tide, hypno-tizing Peg with the motion. She closed her eyes and drifted, hear-ing nothing but the sound of the water whooshing around her.

Had she opened her eyes she would have seen the giant manatee lumbering below searching for sea grass.

Had she not been so lulled into a trance, she would have noticed the curious elephantine creature approaching the dangling green seat cushion straps.

Had she felt the strong tug on the cushion, she would have sensed the beast's prehistoric teeth clamped to the cushion strap.

And he was underneath her. Skin to hide.

Peg screamed and flailed, clutching the seat cushion, but the manatee refused to give up its lunch. Off they went on a Key West sleigh ride at a speed that would have impressed the most discern-ing audience at Sea World. Peg on its back, the spooked manatee darted and weaved and dived under the water.

... can't breathe...

The two-headed monster resurfaced with an unnatural, guttural wail: "HELP..."

... under the water...

The sound cut off as they submerged yet again.

"MEEEE..."

... gonna die...

After some distance, the manatee decided to find less noisy greener pastures and let go, plunking Peg right into the side of the Florida Fish and Wildlife Commission boat – *State Law Enforcement* written in bold letters on the side.

Gasping for breath, Peg looked up at the uniformed men in the boat.

"Thank God. You saved me. I almost died." She had lost the mask and snorkel somewhere along the way.

An imposing man in khaki said, "Ma'am, we're gonna need you to get out of the water. Per the laws that protect Florida's wildlife, you're under arrest for the molestation of a sea creature." He put down the ladder for her to climb up.

"What? Molestation? It molested *me*." Peg thrashed her way to the ladder and clung to it.

"Ma'am, we're gonna need your cooperation here." He offered his big, hairy arm.

Peg observed the gun in the holster as she took his hand. "I am cooperating. I am a cooperative person. I would never molest anything."

One of the other officers whispered to another, "Yeah, right, lady. As far as we know that manatee is smoking a cigarette 50 yards from here." They snickered.

He hoisted her dripping butt out of the water. The effort made her belch in very close proximity to the officer's face.

"Have you been drinking, ma'am?"

"Um no... I mean yes... if you count champagne as drinking... I'm old enough though... you can probably tell..."

"We're gonna take you in. It is a federal offence to touch a manatee. Could be six months jail sentence. Hefty fines too." The officer showed her where to sit in the boat.

"Six MONTHS? Don't drug runners get less than that?"

"It's harassment, ma'am."

"I didn't touch it. I mean I *touched* it after it dragged me... I can't go with you, my friends are over in that boat." She could see Randolph standing with his hands in the air. He looked annoyed.

Before she knew it, the FWC boat kicked into high gear. "Not my fault," she screamed to no avail. The engines blocked out all conversation. Her hair whipped around her head flinging remnants of seawater and hot-caramel-auburn throughout the boat. Tears flowed, adding to the liquids jettisoning around her. "I can't go to jail. I have a dog... he needs me. I've never even had a speeding ticket. I would never be mean to an animal. Sure, I eat meat... I know that's pretty mean... but I feel guilty about it... and it's *not* illegal or anything," she cried.

The officers ignored her. Steering the boat toward the marina, they talked among themselves in their earpieces.

Five uniformed Fish and Wildlife officers lined up at the dock. With crossed arms and polarized sunglasses, they made for a formidable group. One towering officer in the middle had his phone to his ear.

Observing her welcome committee as the boat slowed, Peg shook with fear. "I'm not a drug runner. I'm very anti-drugs for that matter." She sobbed her words through more sobbing. Pulling up to the dock she wailed, "I have a dog. He's expecting me home. He'll be worried."

The phone-to-ear-officer stepped forward, then snapped his phone into its belt holster. He leaned over the side of the boat and stretched out his arm. "Give me your hand, ma'am."

"My hands are gross. I've been wiping my nose. I didn't have a tissue." Peg could see herself in the officer's sunglasses.

"Give me your hand, ma'am."

Peg gave him her hand. "I'm so sorry. I'm all by myself... I don't mean right now... I have friends... but my husband brought me here... I'm not from here."

"Are you Nipper's mother?" the officer asked as he helped her out of the boat.

"What? Yes. How do you know?" Peg looked at the officer's badge.

Officer Bernard Smith.

"I'm Lulu's dad. Randolph called me and told me you would be showing up here." He put his arm around Peg. "Let's get you home to your dog."

Peg leaned against him as they walked. He opened the door to the back seat of the car and she got in.

"So I don't have to go to jail?" Peg's face was teary.

"No, ma'am."

"Thank you. I'm Peg, by the way."

"I know, ma'am. Peg from Chicago. Where it's cold."

"Yes."

Text to Randolph

Hi. So sorry about almost going to jail. Hope that didn't ruin your time catching lobsters. Did you get to cook them? Sorry again. Pls thank Bernard for me too.

Text from Randolph

No! I did not get to cook any lobsters! Pierre and I had to go to FWC office.

Text to Randolph

Sorry.

> *Text from Randolph*
>
> ```
> It took too long for Bernie to clear every-
> thing up. No lobster grilling.
> ```

> *Text from Peg*
>
> ```
> So sorry.
> ```

> *Text from Randolph (hours later)*
>
> ```
> Apology accepted.
> ```

Peg pictured him typing those words using only his *middle* fingers.

Friend in Need

Peg paced and glanced out of the NO EXIT sign on the glass door to the Key West airport tarmac. Sun peeked between the dark clouds of the squall. Puddles steamed on the runway as the ground attempted to cool itself to a solid.

"It's so weird to be able to greet people at the gate. I miss this from the old days. Not many airports where you can see the plane land as you wait." Peg chatted in the direction of the bartender setting up drinks at the bar located in front of the arrivals entrance. "The tourists are not going to miss the bar, that's for sure."

The bartender smiled and nodded. "I'm the Key West version of the gift shop in a museum. Gotta go through the bar or you can't get out of the airport." He put his hands on his hips and widened his stance.

Peg smiled at him. "Do you think that the plane will make it in with all of this crazy weather?" She pointed to the blackening sky.

"Sure they will. This is nothin'. The pilots are all navy trained. They like a little bit of wind shear." The bartender took a quick look outside then added a few more cups to the counter before pouring generous amounts of tequila across the line of beverages.

"It looks so dark over the runway. Don't they land from that direction?"

"You need this." He held up the cup and the green liquid sloshed around. "Drink one and you'll forget your worries. Drink two – you'll forget your manners. Drink three – you'll forget your spouse." He pointed to the ring-less tan line around the fourth finger of his left hand.

Peg blushed then paled.

I wonder how many of these Clark drank before flying to Cuba?

"No… I'm fine." She chewed the skin on the outside of her pinky nail. "I'm just excited to see my friend who's coming from Chicago. I haven't seen her in months. I really need her to get here. She's my best friend. This kind of weather would have shut down O'Hare. I mean, they're pretty good in the winter with the snow and ice, but they're very cautious with lightning and wind. There was that terrible plane crash back in the—"

"It's on the house." He came around the bar and shoved the drink into Peg's hand. "Take a big sip."

Outside the window a black cloud engulfed the airport. Rain pelted the door. Peg took a swig. The lime medicine coated her throat and nerves.

This shouldn't taste this good.

A dim hum could be heard, a sputtering plane engine sound interspersed with thunder. Peg stood on tiptoes and craned her neck to see the plane emerge as a blurry vision through the window waterfall. The propellers whirred with 70 years of muscle memory, guiding the plane off the airstrip to the middle of the tarmac. The pilot cut the engines 100 yards away from the entrance. Water careened off of the welcome-mannequins' backs as they braved the elements.

"She's here." Peg beamed.

The bartender whoo-whooed. "Yessss."

The poncho'd maintenance workers wheeled the metal stairs to the airplane door. Rain poured while lightning bolted and the airplane door opened.

"Is this safe? I mean… a metal stairway and lightning? The people are going to get soaked, if they don't die first." Peg's voice pitched higher as she spoke. "They're pretty far away. Don't they wait to let the people off till it stops raining?"

The bartender gave her a look, then motioned with a "take a drink" hand.

Eyes glued to the door, Peg complied.

The passengers exited the plane to a torrent of rain, feet slipping on the steps as they descended. Purses, computer bags and newspapers held overhead in a struggle to defend themselves against a very wet and angry Mother Nature. One by one they ran into the terminal, leaving no bit of clothing or free-carry-on undrenched. Peg scrutinized each of the running passengers, searching for the familiar horn-rimmed glasses and spiky hair.

She heard her before she could see her.

"Fucking fuckity fuck fucker." Trudy ran through the door. The wheels of her bedraggled carry-on suitcase flung water behind her. Squinting, she held her dripping, foggy glasses by the frame and, with a Labrador head-shake, she stomped past the electronic doors, into the meet and greet area.

"You're HERE. With ME." Peg ambushed her unsuspecting wet friend. She picked Trudy up and twirled her with such force that Trudy's glasses hurled out of her hand and flung over the crowd, skimming across the bar.

Trudy continued her rant. "I've never seen rain like that before. The SOBs don't even give you an umbrella. What kind of a miserable–"

Peg embraced her wet buddy. "You made it. You're soaked." She held her at arm's length. "Let me look at you. It's really you. Hey, where are your glasses?"

Trudy screwed up her eyes. "Most likely being worn by a passing fish, my God, that's a lot of water." She returned the hug.

The bartender hooted his greeting. "Welcome, best friend who we've been so worried about." He held up Trudy's specs in one hand and a cup of green liquid in the other. "Glasses," he presented both to Trudy, "are my specialty."

Peg took her cup from the counter. "I'm already half-finished with mine."

"I love this guy." Trudy placed the glasses on her nose. She winked at the bartender as she chugged the entire contents in one giant gulp. "Two more for the road, my good man." Trudy took out her purse and put down three soggy twenty-dollar bills. She handed a pre-made drink from the line-up to Peg and kept one for herself. "Let's go. I can't wait to see Nipper."

Peg and Trudy left the airport, their drinking arms linked. "Jeez, that was a quick storm. It couldn't'ta waited 15 minutes for us to get out of the plane." Trudy pointed to the sun peeking out through ominous clouds, her glasses fogged as they exited the air conditioning.

"Ha, get used to that." Peg chuckled. "Oh, and watch out for the chickens." She shooed away a rooster who stood his ground next to the curb. "They're everywhere and definitely follow the motto *It's five am somewhere.* Ha, I read that on a tee shirt. That's the *nicest* thing I've ever read on a tee shirt in Key West, believe me. There's this one with a stick figure kneeling behind another one... can't *un*-see that." Peg snuggled her friend. "Oh, I can't believe you're really here." She wrapped her arm around Trudy's shoulders.

"What kind of an original Wright brothers' plane did I come in on? For real, the propellers started and stopped in midair, diving, bobbing and weaving." Trudy rolled her head from side to side. "The guy next to me turned the color of this drink." Trudy raised the cup to her mouth as she walked. "My God, it's hell-hot here." She swilled the beverage.

"I know. People say you get used to it. I do have a rash that has acclimated nicely." She scratched under her right breast.

"I can see how yeasts would thrive." Trudy wiped her cheek with her wet sleeve. "Where's the car?"

"I had to take a taxi to the airport. I have a flat tire and haven't fixed it yet. I think the rubber melted into the street. Clark usually handles the car stuff."

"Asshole."

Peg changed the subject. "It's okay though, I don't need the car. It's easy to walk everywhere. I could've walked to the airport but the storm freaked me out."

Trudy held on to her baseball cap in the wind. "You're not in Kansas anymore, Dorothy."

They jumped into a cab. "Cheers." Peg thudded her cup to Trudy's and they downed the liquid.

The angry sky blackened on the horizon as another squall gained strength. But over the cab, the sun's rays beamed in the patchy blue sky. The taxi careened through a considerable amount of standing water on the streets, splashing cursing tourists who crossed the road to the beach.

"Sorry, mon," the taxi driver yelled out the window. "Too much rain. Can't be elped."

Trudy closed her window to avoid a re-soaking. "Shit."

Peg laughed. "I know, the island's made of coral. The water takes a while to soak back into the ground after these big rains."

"Man, if it looks like this after a short rainstorm, I can't imagine what it'd look like after a hurricane."

Argh. Hurricanes. Don't think about the grotto… not your fault… it's Africa's fault…

"Here we are. Home sweet home." The cab stopped next to the gate. Nipper heard the sound of the gravel as the cab pulled up. He barked wildly.

"Where's my baby? My good boy?" Trudy called out to the dog. Peg opened the gate and went back to the taxi to pay and grab the suitcase. The dog jumped at the glass door until Trudy burst in, and then he power-bounded into her stomach. "Ugh. Okay. Okay. I know. You must smell your old buddy Tucker. He wishes he could be here instead of with the stoner next-door neighbor kid." She knelt down laughing while the dog licked her face. "Tucker loves that kid though. I'll text him to see how they're doing. Probably getting high together."

"I wish you could've brought Tucker too. Can you tell that Nipper and I missed you?" Peg joined in the human/canine melee. The inside air felt cool and moist. Condensation obscured the windows. "She's here, Nipper. It's real. I can't believe that you're really HERE." Peg lifted Trudy off of the floor and the dog wiggled and waggled in-between their legs.

"I can't believe that you really LIVE here." Trudy took in the surroundings. "Two questions. One. Where is your dryer so that I can peel off these soaking clothes? Two. Where is the liquor in this tiny house?"

Peg beamed. "I'm so happy that you're here. Okay. First answer, the dryer is in the closet behind you. I know, it's in the kitchen, but I'm lucky to be able to do laundry inside the house. Most people go to the laundromat or do their washing outside."

"Jesus, it's the 21st century, people." Trudy opened a closet door and gave Peg a quizzical look. The closet shelves were lined with canned goods and bottles, each with its own specific label.

"Not that one, the one next to it."

Trudy held up a can.

"I know, I know." Peg scrunched her face.

"The tomato soup has a label on it that says *Tomato Soup*. Is everything in alphabetical order?"

"I got a new label maker… it's been a long month… and it's an addiction… honestly, I couldn't stop."

"No label making for you this week. We're two women on the town." Trudy placed the can back next to the clearly marked *Tortilla Soup*.

Peg whooped and opened the fridge, "Second answer is champagne is chillin'." She presented the green bottle. "Voilà."

"Learning French for any particular reason?"

"Shut up. I'm not looking for another man. And even if I was, the *Canadian* has a sea nymph for a girlfriend. I mean it. The real thing. Fins and gills. With giant boobs. And, I haven't spoken to him since the… you know. Manatee situation." Peg's voice went to a whisper and she looked around.

Trudy smiled and held up her bubbling champagne glass. "Cheers, a perfect way to prepare for an evening of drinking. Maybe after we drink this, you can teach me how to ride a manatee." Trudy thrust her pelvis back and forth.

Peg held her fingers to her lips. "Shut up, it's serious. I could have gone to jail." She swung at her friend and giggled. "Ooo, this stuff is good, do you want to stay in or go out?"

"Let's go out. Lady I work with said that I gotta go to Duval Street. Something about Captain Tony's, and a Green Parrot."

"Yay! A Duval crawl. I haven't done that yet. Seemed weird to do it by myself." She turned to Trudy, "Why don't you move here? We can do everything together. Just quit your job and move to Key West," she pleaded with prayer hands.

"What about if Clark comes back? I'll have to make good on my promise to kill him. Then I'd go to jail and I don't think that your Fish and Wildlife officer would be able to get me out of that one." Trudy poured herself another libation.

"So, you are considering it then?" Peg's nose snorted a laugh.

"We'll see. We have a week to drink it… I mean think it over."
Trudy cheers-ed the air.

"I'm so happy now that you're here." Peg wheeled the suitcase
into the spare bedroom. "I'll give Nipper a walk and you change
your clothes. Wear something cool, and I don't mean fashionable.
Prepare to sweat. We'll walk to our crawl." Peg jingled the leash.
"C'mere, Nipper."

"Whooo… paaarrrttaaayy." Trudy performed a combination of
the hustle and the jig down the hall, drink sloshing.

Peg and Nipper strode out into the warm gusts of wind – no
rain, but blustery and hot. "Nipper, I'll give you your special treats
while Trudy and I are out tonight." The dog perked up his ears
when he heard the word *treats* then continued on to do his business in all of the regular spots along the walk.

They returned to find both Trudy and her beverage refreshed.

Waving goodbye to the contented dog, they closed the gate and
turned down the street.

"How far are we walking?" Trudy surveyed the tumultuous sky.

"Everything is pretty clo–" Peg stopped talking and covered her
mouth with her hand. She turned and covered Trudy's mouth
with her other hand.

"Mmmm, mmm." Trudy peeled Peg's hand off of her mouth.

"What on earth are you doing?"

"Cover your mouth," Peg mumbled underneath her own fingers. "It's dragonfly season." A swarm of buzzing, winged insects
flew helter-skelter around them.

One zinged into Trudy's face. "Holy shit." She covered her
mouth.

"I don't care how much protein they have. Take it from me. It's
an unwanted snack." Peg talked into the palm of her hand until a
blustery breeze carried the mob of black bugs down the street. "It's
okay. You can put your hand down. They're gone, for now."

Trudy did a 360-degree spin around to make sure that the
coast was clear. A straggler whizzed by. Returning hand to mouth
Trudy declared, "I need another drink."

"Lots of bars and other stuff to see in Key West. The buoy that

marks the Southernmost Point, tons of museums and galleries..."
Peg's voice was drowned out by the Ghosts and Graveyards bus
tour coming from behind them on the street. Words like *death,*
corpse and *haints* echoed out as the tour guide spoke.

Peg shivered.

...haints...

As if on cue, the bus passengers yelled in their direction, "You're
doomed."

Amused, Trudy yelled back, "No. *You're* doomed."

Peg shushed Trudy. "I don't think anyone should be joking
around like that. I mean... I know that it's not really true...
that we're doomed... but I don't like to hear it anyway... cause
if something bad does happen... then naturally I'll think I *am*
doomed and it might just be a coincidence... and..."

"Whoa there." Trudy stopped short. "What are you talking
about? You know it's all a joke. Right?"

"I know. Of course. I know." Peg took a deep breath.

"Who needs a drink now?" Trudy held her friend around the
waist and pressed forward at a faster clip.

A voice sang out from a bicyclist across the street, "I do, ladies."
Wearing a thong with black fishnet stockings, turquoise bustier
with matching top hat, he sat up stick straight in order to reach
the Easy Rider handlebars. Before the women had a chance to
respond, he tipped his top hat and disappeared into the next driveway.

"What the?" They giggled with faces close together.

"This is why I need you here... as a witness. No one would
believe me."

They re-linked sweaty elbows.

"How much longer? The wick-away in this shirt has up and
left." A gust of hot air almost knocked her over. "This is some
wind." Newspapers and garbage danced in whirlpools in the alleys.

"Gale force... ridiculously strong tonight." Peg supported her
friend's back and pushed her forward. "Almost there."

"Let's start at Captain Tony's. It used to be Sloppy Joe's but now
Sloppy Joe's is there." Peg pointed across the street to the open

windows filled to overflow with tourists screaming along with the band, "Why don't we get drunk and screw?"

"Jimmy Buffett is a god here," Peg whispered.

"Right. Some god. Get drunk and get screwed buying all of his crap," Trudy said too loud.

"Shhh. You'll start a riot."

"I mean, look at those people. All dressed the same with their hands in the air. Probably how Hitler got started."

Peg laughed. "Let's go before you start another world war. I didn't know you were so anti-Margaritaville." She hugged Trudy to distract her. "On a history note, there's a story about Hemingway taking the urinal from Captain Tony's when they moved the bar. He said that he *pissed away* so much money into the urinal that he owned it."

"I just hope he didn't take the toilet in the ladies' room, 'cause I gotta go." Trudy quickened her step and crossed against the light on Duval Street. A scooter honked. She about-faced with both middle fingers flying. "Suck on these birds you parrot-headed mother fu–"

"Let's go." Peg grabbed one of Trudy's obscene gestures, leaving the other one firmly in position. Trudy sidestepped in front of the scooter and stared down the double-chinned, large-bellied driver.

"Looks like he's had too many cheeseburgers in paradise," Trudy added.

"Okay, okay… I get it." Peg dragged her friend toward the bar entrance.

"I'm just sayin' – definitely not wasting away."

Peg shoved her friend in the door of Captain Tony's. "And… we're here. You go pee and I'll get us some drinks."

Trudy jogged in the direction of the restroom sign. Peg found a couple of spots at the bar. The densely tattooed bartender slapped his hands down on the bar in front of her, "What'll it be, miss? Margaritas are our specialty."

"No. I mean… no thank you. Two rum and Cokes, please."

He looked surprised. "Don't like tequila?"

"Tequila's fine, but don't mention the word *margarita* to my best friend, Trudy. Take my word for it."

"Rum and Cokes. Got it." He continued talking while he mixed the drinks. "Where you from?"

"I live here now but I'm from Chicago."

"You're local? Tonight it's buy one get one free for locals." He placed four drinks in front of her. "Chicago, huh? Never been. I hear it's cold up there."

Before Peg could respond, the bartender was called away on another drink order. Trudy sat down next to her. "Expecting company?" she asked Peg when she noticed the number of drinks lined up.

"Two for one, because I'm local. I'll never get used to saying that." Peg shook her head and shrugged her shoulders.

"I, for one, right at this minute in time, am happy that you are a local." Trudy picked up both of her drinks and clinked them together.

"I, for one, am happy that you are here with me." Peg clinked her two glasses to Trudy's.

"As the seafaring folk say, down the hatch."

Summoned by the nearly empty drinks, the bartender reappeared with two fresh ones. "Welcome," he addressed Trudy with a bow.

"Thank you. Why's there a tree in the middle of the bar? I can figure out why the walls are decorated with bras." Trudy sat up straight. "A bra can get pretty confining after several of these." She lifted her replenished drink.

"Used to be an ice house, then a morgue. During a hurricane, the bodies washed out of the building. That's a hanging tree where 18 people were hanged."

... hurricane... floating corpses...

Peg turned her goose-fleshed neck sideways so that she couldn't see the tree.

"Really? Nice. What's up with the bathroom? Why do the lights flicker blue?" Trudy took a big swig.

"No way. Blue? You saw blue?" His eyes went wide.

"Yeah – a blue light flashed. Like a blue light special or something? More free drinks?" Trudy danced her cup in the air.

Peg laughed until she saw the look on the bartender's face. "What's the matter?"

"That's the Lady in Blue. You saw the Lady in Blue." He was excited.

"I didn't see any lady – only blue," Trudy corrected.

"That's her. She was there with you."

"Who was?" Trudy persisted.

"The ghost that haunts the building. She murdered her family and they hanged her from that tree. People are always trying to get her to come out. It's really rare." The bartender called out to the manager, "Hey boss, there's been a Lady in Blue sighting in the bathroom." He rang the bell hanging on the post in the middle of the bar.

The older man rubbed his hands together. "That's great. We were thinking she'd return. Are you sure it wasn't the other ghost? You know, the woman that killed her baby in the bathroom when she caught her husband up to no good? There'd be a blast of cold air if she was around."

The men turned their attention to Trudy.

"Nope. No blast of cold air. God knows I would have welcomed any air conditioning, no matter what spirit world it came from."

Peg gulped her drink.

"People say the ghosts turn up to give out warnings. I say – the next round of drinks is on the house." The boss–man circled his hand like a lasso and four glasses appeared on the bar in front of the women.

"I don't like this. I think that we should go." Peg fidgeted in her seat and sorted through her wallet to settle up.

Trudy snatched Peg's wallet. "First of all, I'm paying. Second of all, we're not done with our drinks."

Peg's eyes welled up and she leaned closer to Trudy. "I didn't want to tell you this, but the ghosts are after me. They visited me one night when I was sleeping."

Trudy's eyes widened. "What are you talking about? The potty ghosts are in your house too?"

Peg shook her head. "No, different ones. They're called haints. The blue paint on the front porch was chipped and... um... they came to talk to me in the middle of the night and warn me something about Clark."

"Smart haints." Trudy's smirk faded when she saw Peg's hand shaking. "Oh my God, you're really frightened. This isn't a joke to you."

Peg looked down, trying not to cry. However, fueled by alcohol and the proximity of her best friend, the tears flowed freely. The bartender approached them, took one glance at Peg, then quickly about-faced.

"I don't know what's the matter with me. I'm trying to be strong and do this whole new adventure thing, but it's hard and I'm scared and I'm all alone." The choking sobs increased as Peg spoke.

Trudy hugged her friend. "You're not alone. I'm here."

"I know and I'm so happy that you're here," she cried harder, "but you're gonna leave and I'm gonna still be here... alone." Her shoulders heaved up and down.

Trudy held Peg's face in her hands and used her thumbs to wipe away the tears. "Look at me. I'm not gonna leave you. I won't do it. Tucker and I will move here to be with you. I miss you too. We'll rent something at first and then look around to buy."

Peg red-eyed her friend in disbelief. "Really? You're serious? You're not saying this 'cause we've had 15 drinks... right?" She smiled through her remaining tears. "For real?"

"Sure. I'll figure it out. They need accountants here. Right? Why not?" Trudy's eyes glistened under her glasses.

"Why not?" Peg blew her nose with a bar napkin. "We'll all be together again. The four of us on our daily walks, just like old times." She tipped herself off the barstool and bear-hugged Trudy.

Trudy returned the big hug. "I'll drink to that. To our future."

Ceremoniously, they double-clinked their glasses.

The bartender reappeared with four shots of tequila. "Tequila is the happy booze. I thought you might wanna change it up." He handed Peg the box of tissues from the other counter. "I'm having trouble knowin' if I should console or congratulate."

"Thank you. I'm sorry, I'm usually not like this... but I'm fine now because my best friend is moving here... for real... she's gonna do it."

"It's true. I'm gonna do it." Trudy held up the shot glass.

"I'll drink to that too." The bartender filled a shot for himself and raised his glass to Trudy. "May the wind be always at your back. Cheers."

They emptied their glasses.

The dusty fan oscillated in the corner of the bar next to a guitar player. His long hair blew alternately in, then out, of his mouth as he sang. The crowd grew louder as it increased in size and alcohol intake. The friendly bartender hustled into work mode while customers lined up to place their orders.

Trudy folded several bills under her shot glass. "Getting too crowded in here."

"Right. Let's go." Peg swilled the last sip and stood up.

They waved to the bartender, who saluted them as they left.

Peg clasped Trudy's hand and swung her arm up and down. "WHOOO. I'M SO HAPPY," Peg yelled into the blustery wind.

Trudy swiveled her hips in rhythm with her arms. "WHOOO. I'M SO HAPPY TOO."

"I wanna show you this cool neighborhood. It's called the Annex and it's so perfect... almost like it's pretend. Nipper and I walk there."

"Okay, neighbor." Trudy and Peg ringed-around-the-rosy in full giggle.

Holding hands, they skipped down the palm tree-lined street.

Had they not been dancing, and had they been sober, they might have noticed that: the wind increased in both speed and intensity; the coconuts ceased to be hanging on branches; the wind blew at their backs.

THWACK.

Trudy fell.

Peg tripped over her downed friend.

The coconut rolled onto the road.

"Trudy... Trudy... Are you all right?" Peg crawled along the sidewalk to her motionless friend. She picked up Trudy's head and blood flowed freely from the back. "Trudy... Speak to me. Oh my God... No, this can't be... NO."

She yanked her phone from her pocket and dialed 911 with unsteady fingers. "An emergency... a coconut... my friend... please help... I'm in the Annex... the main street... hurry."

Without a second thought, Peg whipped the shirt off her own back, revealing a sweat-stained exercise bra. She crumpled the wick-away shirt and held it to Trudy's bloody head.

Not working... won't absorb...

She cradled Trudy in her arms and whispered in her ear, "You're gonna be okay... we're gonna be neighbors... you're gonna be okay."

The ambulance sirens wailed around the corner and grew louder until the vehicle came to a stop, lights flashing next to the curb. Two EMTs leapt out. One opened the back door of the ambulance for the stretcher, the other grabbed a medical kit and rushed to Peg.

"Lie down, miss. You have blood all over you. Can you speak? Where are you hurt?"

Trudy's head resting on her lap, Peg looked down at her now-bloody exercise bra. "No, not me, it's my best friend... hit on the head with a coconut... still breathing... not talking."

"Let me take a look at her." He knelt down and Peg moved aside.

Carefully lifting Trudy's head, he leaned over to examine her. Rivers of blood fell from the balled-up moisture-resistant shirt. He opened up some heavy gauze and wrapped it around and around and around her head.

"She's gonna be okay, right? She got here today... a few hours ago. But she's gonna move here... to be with me." Peg grabbed his shirt.

"Settle down, ma'am. We're gonna do everything we can.

Please sit down." He disconnected Peg's hands from his neckline. Bloody fingermarks stained his collar.

The other EMT came forward with the stretcher and placed it next to Trudy. "What happened?"

"Another coconut to the head. That's the third one today." He turned to Peg and asked while pointing, "Is this the coconut here?"

"Yes, I think that's the one. Or maybe it was the one to the left... I'm not sure... Does it matter?" Peg rubbed her goose-bumped arms.

"I'll take both of them. They'll use them to analyze strength of impact." He turned to his partner and said, "Give me a blanket. She's in shock." He covered up a shivering Peg with the blanket.

"She got any ID?"

"Trudy. Her name is Trudy Stanislowski." Peg stared down at her limp best friend.

"Okay. Does Trudy have a photo ID?"

"I think so... in her back pocket. Hurry... can't you help her?" Peg begged.

"I don't want to move her. We'll get it once she's immobilized." Both EMTs nodded in agreement.

The uniformed men carefully slid the stretcher under Trudy's body and fastened the straps.

"On three." The men grasped the stretcher's handles. "One, two, three."

Trudy levitated into the ambulance. One EMT followed her into the vehicle while the other stabilized the medical equipment so that the doors could close.

Peg cried, "I'm going in there with her... not leaving her alone." She threw the blanket off, scrambled to stand, then staggered to the ambulance.

The EMT intercepted Peg. "Ma'am, we can't take you in the back of the vehicle, but you can ride in front." He picked up the blanket from the ground and guided her to the passenger door.

Peg resisted and ran to the back of the ambulance again. "I need to be with her... when she wakes up... I want her to see me." The EMT inside the ambulance closed the door. Peg stood on the bumper and suction-cupped her hands to the glass. "Trudy, I'm here. I won't leave you." Peg pressed her face to the window.

"Ma'am, come with me. We'll be at the hospital in five minutes. The faster you cooperate, the faster we can get help for your friend." He offered the blanket back to Peg and motioned toward the front of the vehicle.

Peg looked in the window then back at the EMT. "I'll be here, Trudy. I'm with you… in the front." Peg patted the side of the ambulance and stepped off of the bumper. The driver rewrapped the blanket around her shoulders and opened the passenger door.

Once seated, Peg sobbed as the engine started. "It's all my fault… bus people said we're doomed… took her to a haunted bar…" sniff, gasp, "…the lady ghost in the potty warned her…" sniffle, snort, "…Trudy said she'd move here…" chortle, wheeze, "…the bartender toasted us… wind to our backs…" deep breath, "…it was to our backs all right… bastard…"

"We're at the hospital, ma'am." The driver bolted out of the door.

Disoriented and bedraggled, Peg zigzagged out to meet the medical entourage that surrounded Trudy at the back of the ambulance. To their right, Peg saw the emergency room. To their left, she heard a helicopter's whirling blades.

The group circled Trudy like ants.

"What happened?"

"Coconut."

"To the head?"

"Yeah."

"Better write it on her so they know how it happened."

"Right." He took out a marker and wrote COCONUT in big black letters across Trudy's forehead under the white gauze.

A doctor bellowed a command over the commotion. The pod of white coats, and Trudy, proceeded to the left.

"Where's she going? Why aren't you taking her into the hospital?" Peg grabbed the doctor's coat sleeve.

"It's a potential brain injury. We don't handle them here. She's being life-flighted to Miami." He shouted to the pilot who walked past them, "Another nut case." The pilot saluted and continued toward the helicopter. The doctor noticed Peg's bloodstained bra. "Are you bleeding? This lady's bleeding. Help her STAT."

"What? NO." Peg shrugged off the nurse who approached her. "Miami? What are you talking about? She can't go to Miami. She's staying here with me." Peg ran toward the helicopter. "TRUDY... TRUDY..."

The wind from the blades spun Peg's hair into gravity-defying tentacles. Moving forward, she leaned her body into the force of the blasts.

The nurse reached through the hairdo maelstrom and pulled her back.

Peg saw Trudy through the large window of the helicopter. The orange straps cocooned her friend's body. The white bandage mummified the top of her head with the letters "N-U-T" exposed on the right side of her forehead. One of the coconuts was strapped next to Trudy's breast, creating the illusion that she wore a tropical brassiere on her chopper ride out of Key West.

The helicopter lifted into the air.

"Noooooo." Peg fell to the ground.

The nurse stooped down. "Let's get you inside."

Peg knelt on the concrete until the sound of the helicopter blades faded out of earshot.

"Come on. I'll get you a shirt to put on." Supporting Peg's elbow, the nurse helped her to her feet. They walked together through the emergency room entrance.

"Are you sure you don't need medical attention?" the nurse asked as she rummaged through a box of clothes marked *clean*. She handed Peg a fluorescent yellow tee shirt.

"No, I need to know where my friend is going. I have to be with her." Peg tugged the shirt over her bloodstained bra. It said *Will work for beer*.

"I'm sorry, it's all I could find," the nurse said.

"Could be worse... the shirt... I mean... not my life... *that*... actually... could not be worse." Peg held out her hands. Her nails were crusted with rusty dried blood.

"Are you related to the patient?"

"No, I'm her best friend."

"Then, due to privacy laws, the dispatcher and staff won't give out any details about where she's going."

Peg slumped. "But I'm like a relative... closer than a relative."

"Go home and get some sleep. You'll feel better in the morning. Do you have a ride?"

Peg shook her head and whispered, "No."

The nurse nodded to the woman behind the desk. "Call Conch Taxi Service."

The excitement, disappointment, alcohol, fear and sadness caught up with Peg. "My best friend... she's not coming back here, is she?"

"No, she's not," the nurse replied, then disappeared through the door.

"Cab for one?" asked the woman on the phone.

"Yes, I'm alone."

Finding Trudy

Day One (post coconut)

"As I said before, ma'am, I can NOT give out any information about your friend. The only thing I can tell you is that she is no longer at this facility," the hospital admissions director snipped in a not-so-patient voice.

"The Life Flight people said that they took her to your hospital. She must be there," Peg pleaded in a desperate tone.

"Ma'am. She was here and then, based on her condition, she was transferred elsewhere. That's ALL I can say. I need to attend to other patients now. Goodbye."

The line clicked off. Peg held the disconnected phone up to her head while it beeped, not wanting to hang up. Maybe the woman would start speaking again. Maybe she would feel sorry for Peg. Maybe she would help her find Trudy.

After a couple of minutes, Peg pushed the off button. She held her head in her hands and slumped over the counter.

How can I go to her when I don't know where she is?

Text from Peg to Clark

Call me. It's an emergency. I'm fine but Trudy's not. I need your help.

Email from Peg to Clark

Clark – I know that you don't get the emails I send until days later, but PLEASE call me as soon as you get this. I need your help.

> Trudy was here and got hit on the head with a coconut and knocked out. I don't know how she is. They life-flighted her by helicopter to Miami. The Miami hospital sent her somewhere else and they won't tell me where. How can I find out where she is? I can't do *nothing*, but that's what I'm doing. I am alone in Key West and need you.
>
> Please, please, please call me.

Peg hit the send button and stared at the screen, willing it to respond. Nothing.

Think… think… Who can I contact?

The teenage neighbor boy who is watching Trudy's dog, Tucker.

Peg scrolled through her old Rolodex for the boy's number. She shook off the wave of nostalgia as she touched each well-worn index card from her past life.

Phone call to teenage neighbor boy

Boy: "Hullo?"

Peg: "Hi, this is Peg. I'm a friend of Trudy's. She got hurt and I'm wondering if you have heard from her or anyone who would know about her?"

Boy: "Uh – she's in Key West."

Peg: "Right. I'm in Key West and she *was* with me, but she was injured and helicoptered to Miami and then somewhere else… I just don't know where."

Boy: "Dude. That sucks."

Peg could hear the machine-gun fire of a video game in the background.

Peg: "Yes, that does suck. You haven't heard from anyone? No phone calls… maybe to your mother?"

> Boy: "Uh. No. The dog's cool though."
>
> Peg: "I'm sure that you are taking good care of him. Keep my number in case you hear from anyone."
>
> Boy: "No prob. Later."
>
> Peg: "Any news… at all from any…"

Click.

Peg rolled onto the floor and curled up into a ball. The dog licked her ear.

Think.

You have to think.

What about her sister? They haven't spoken to each other in years… but maybe, since she is a relative, someone contacted her…

She crawled to the desk and lifted the Rolodex to the floor. Sitting cross-legged on the floor, she took a deep breath and dialed the number on the card.

> *Phone call to Trudy's sister*
>
> Peg: "Hi, this is Trudy's friend Peg. Has anyone contacted you about Trudy? She's been injured and I don't know where she is."
>
> Sister: "Is she dead?"
>
> Peg: "No. Oh my God, no… she's…"
>
> Sister: "Then I don't care."
>
> Peg: "I just thought that–"

The line disconnected.

Peg tossed the phone across the floor. It spun round and round until it smacked into the wall. Nipper jumped up at the noise and looked expectantly at Peg, who lay flat on her back with her eyes closed. The dog gazed down at her face and licked her nose. When there was no reaction from Peg, he licked again. With this rare green light to perform a thorough nostril cleaning, he placed both front paws on her chest, curled his tongue and dug in.

Sputtering, she pushed the dog off. "Okay, okay, I'll get up." She turned onto her hands and knees then rose to her feet to retrieve her phone. Peg followed Nipper, who ran into the guest bedroom where Trudy's suitcase lay open on the floor. The wet clothes from the day before hung, still wet, over the arm of the chair. Peg flopped backward on top of the guest bed, covering her nose when Nipper hopped up next to her. Holding the dog at arm's length she said to the ceiling, "Trudy, I won't abandon you. If I have to call all of the hospitals in Florida and then all of the hospitals in the country, I will find you."

Her phone buzzed. Her heart leapt.

Text from Clark

```
Can't call right now. Swamped. Trudy will be
fine - she'll show up.
```

Text to Clark

```
Show up? She's unconscious.
Get home now or I'm outta here.
```

Text from Clark

```
I'm emailing you the contract from the Cuban
subsidiary so you can see the importance of
this mission. We're going into the mountains
```

> for a few weeks. After that, I'll come home.
> I promise.

Peg sighed when she saw the email come through. It was a real project – signature and everything.

Clark is working to better an entire country and I'm playing the jealous housewife.

Her fingers felt heavy. Her eyelids too huge to keep open. Nipper curled up next to her. The guest bed was occupied but the guest was nowhere to be found.

Day Two, Three, Four... Twenty (post coconut)

Call hospitals
  Lie on floor
  Text Clark
  Erase text to Clark
  Lie on guest bed
  Write email to Clark
  Lie on couch
  Erase email to Clark
  Walk dog
  Drink
  Sleep (sort of)

Day Twenty-One (post coconut)

As the sun set, Nipper Houdinied out of his collar and took off down the street.

"Nipper, come back here." Peg woke from her zombie-walk state, the leash dangling in her hand. The dog greyhounded around the corner then slid to a screeching halt next to the familiar glitzy baby buggy. Peg chased him at full speed for a full ten feet, then paused to put her hands on her knees to catch her breath. Panting, she continued her pursuit but slowed when she saw Randolph place Lulu on the ground to greet Nipper.

Peg limp-walked up to them with her fingers pressed under her ribcage. She gasped for air. "I need to get more cardio. Hi, Randolph. Hi, Lulu." She slipped the collar over her renegade dog's head.

Randolph looked sideways as he spoke. His voice frosty. "Hi, Peg. You really need to keep a better grip on your dog. He's going to get hurt if he keeps doing this you know and–" He spun to face her to continue, then hesitated. "Oh my. You look terrible." He moved closer to get a better look. "Are you okay?" He poked her cheek with his pointer finger.

Peg welled up. "No." She avoided his eyes.

Randolph thawed. "What's the matter, doll?"

Looking down, the tears trickled. "I can't find my friend. She was hit on the head by a falling coconut and airlifted out of here. I've called every hospital in five states and I can't find her. Either they won't tell me... or won't talk to me." She choked. "I'm so worried."

Lulu sat under Nipper's front legs as he groomed the top of her head.

Randolph put his arm over Peg's shoulder. "I'm sure that your friend is okay. I mean at least you know the helicopter worked. She got out of here – right? That's not always the case. I knew a guy, and, well, when they couldn't get the helicopter started–"

Peg sobbed for real. "She's gone. I don't know where she is."

Randolph threw his hands in the air. "Stop. Please. I can't stand the sight of tears. I don't care what Bernie says, I am compassionate. It's a curse." He took a step back. "Is that a stream of snot dripping below your chin?"

Peg gurgled, "I think so." She schwiped her nose back and forth, leaving a zigzaggy goo streak on her forearm.

"Everyone says that I'm too nice. Honestly they're right." He took a tissue out of the zipper pouch on the buggy and handed it to Peg. "Here's what I'll do. I'll talk to Bernie."

"What can he do?" Peg honked a nose blow into the tissue. "Does he do work for the hospitals too?"

"Not exactly, but he might be able to do a search for your friend."

Peg lifted her head. "Really? He would do that? There are privacy laws... and they are so strict–"

"Bernie knows a lot of people. He's very respected." Randolph chest-puffed as he spoke.

"That would be wonderful. Anything... I'll text you the details–"

"No promises," Randolph interrupted. "But he'll try if I ask him."

"Thank you... and..." Peg paused. "I'm sorry about ruining your lobster catching." The tears reformulated.

Peg took a breath to continue. Randolph held up a finger to shush her then pulled it away from her drippy lips before it made contact.

"No talking about it." He did a just-in-case finger cleanse on his shirt.

Peg nodded and wiped each eye with the used tissue.

The dogs were contentedly lying next to each other on the sidewalk. Lulu's head gleamed. A smile formed on Peg's face as she watched the dogs.

Randolph thought for a second, started to speak, then stopped, then started again. "There's a dog float at the Fantasy Fest Parade tomorrow evening."

"Oh," Peg said, "that's nice."

"Yes, and I'm running it. I do all of the creatives for the float."

"You'll be good at that," Peg added, not knowing what else to say.

Randolph blurted, "I've had a cancellation and I'd like for you and Nipper to come on the float. You need to dress alike and you can sit next to Lulu and me."

Peg's numbness prevented any protest. "Sure, that would be great," she lied.

"Super." He patted Peg on the back. "We'll chat."

Randolph picked up Lulu, who bared her teeth when he placed her in the buggy. "You can see your boyfriend later, you diva." Lulu snapped at his finger as he waggled it in front of her nose. He yanked the cover of the stroller shut and wheeled off in the other direction.

Peg walked a couple of steps, but the dog resisted the leash.

"Let's go, Nipper." Peg yanked with greater effort until he reluctantly relented and moved his feet.

"Come on, mister, I can't have *you* leaving me for another woman."

Her stomach twisted at her own words.

Clark... no... not true... stop thinking about it. Need to think about Fantasy Fest... what am I supposed to do?

To distract herself as they walked, she asked her phone out loud, "Okay, Google. What is Fantasy Fest?"

Google responded in a helpful voice: "Fantasy Fest is a street fair for grown-ups. It brings in more than 100,000 visitors each year to the island of Key West. Body paint and imagination are a must."

Wow, 100,000 body-painted people? I can't go out in body paint... not enough Chardonnay in the world.

Back at the house, she Googled images of the Fantasy Fest dog float. It seemed harmless enough. Some of the pets were naked, but their owners were fully dressed in dog costumes. This was a relief, since the image of the "aviary" float showed a woman with breasts painted in the likeness of colorful birds – above the artwork, in black magic marker, the word *swallows*.

Thank God I don't have a parakeet... the bird float?... no thank you.

Fantasy Festering

The next day, Peg's heart leapt when she read the text from Randolph.

Text from Randolph

Bernie located your friend, Trudy. He can't say where she is. She can't contact anyone and they won't let you talk to her. Sorry. At least you know that she is alive.

Text from Peg

Is she okay? Can she talk? Does she have permanent damage? How long do you think it will be? Can't Bernie tell me where she is so that I can go there?

Text from Randolph

No.

Text from Peg

Right, of course not. I don't want to get Bernie in trouble.

Text from Randolph

Bernie can't tell you any more. He broke quite a few rules. I won't be able to help *him* if *he* goes to jail.

Text from Peg

No, of course not, I'm so grateful. I'm so relieved that at least *he* knows where she is. Please tell him thank you very much.

Text from Randolph

I will. Also – be at the float site tonight at 6:30 sharp. The Fantasy Fest parade starts at 7:00. Dress like Nipper and don't be late. I had to turn down two French Bulldogs who attempted bribery for your spot on the float.

Text from Peg

I don't want to make anyone mad... if they want my spot...

> **Text from Randolph**
>
> ```
> French Bulldogs aren't real dogs. They have
> to be inseminated artificially - hips too
> small. Only dogs that reproduce naturally
> are invited on the float.
> 6:30. Sharp.
> ```

Yick, that's a horrible thought… an undulating mass of humping dogs floating down the street.

> **Text from Peg**
>
> ```
> We'll be there.
> ```

In the past, she would have shared everything with her husband. Where was he? Why was she alone in this? Clark's silence was deafening. Shaking off her feelings of despair, longing for some control, she re-energized to prepare for Fantasy Fest.

Nipper sat on his haunches with one leg lifted up to his ear. Head down, tongue in full gear, he slurped around the area on his body that had, once upon a time, contained his reproductive equipment.

Peg made a face. "I *guess* you still qualify for the float."

She opened up her laptop and Googled *matching dog and owner costumes*. Scrolling through costume options like Han Solo and Chewbacca, Vendor and Hotdog, and Wicked Witch of the West and Toto, Peg sighed. "Ugh. You won't even wear a bandana. I can't imagine you in a full lion mane." Nipper made eye contact with Peg in affirmation then resumed his task.

"Okay, how about *easy* dog and owner costumes," she asked

herself out loud as she typed. She flipped through the search results and yawned. "I totally don't want to do this." She closed the PC.

Trudy, where are you? Why can't you call me? I just hope you're okay.

Dog-tired and bone-weary, Peg collapsed on the couch. She could hear the distant hoots and hollers from the crowds walking toward Duval Street. Nipper jumped up and plopped his head on her leg, eager for a comfy lap. Peg caressed his velvety ears – so smooth and silky. Her body relaxed. Her breathing slowed. She closed her eyes and slept. It was a dark, dreamless sleep. The shadows cast lower on the wall as the clock tick-tocked.

"Crap. What time is it?" Peg's semi-awake body stood up faster than her bloodstream. Woozily, she sat back down.

She looked at the clock. "Six fifteen? Argghh. We're going to be late." She stood up again, heart pounding. The dog wagged his tail.

"What are we going to wear, Nipper? Or should I say, what am *I* going to wear? You'll be having none of this costume business, smart dog."

Nipper barked.

Peg scurried into the bedroom and opened up the bottom dresser drawer to its fullest two inches. She yanked out assorted clothes and chucked them onto the bed. Sifting through the pile, she picked out a pair of brown leggings and a brown bodysuit that snapped at the crotch. A flashback ensued: she'd worn the donkey head at the office Halloween party and Clark had followed behind her in the hindquarters.

If Trudy were here she would say, "If the ass fits..." I miss her.

She tugged the 15-year-old leggings over her thighs and shimmied them around her hips. Her stomach formed a round pillow in the spandex-free stockings.

My God, I think this waistband is made of scrap metal... it's cutting me in half...

Not having the time to fuss about self-mutilation, she pulled the one-piece bodysuit over her head. Leaning forward, she reached one arm between her legs to catch the snaps on the flap at her fanny. Yet, the farther she bent over to grab them, the higher the snaps scooched up her back.

...like a dog chasing his tail...

Not having the time to snap-catch, she checked herself out in the mirror.

A pregnant dog with a floppy metal tail.

She split her hair into two fluffy pigtails, sticking straight up like ears on the top of her head. Nipper's old collar smelled like three years of wet dog, but she loosened it and clicked it around her neck. The crusty, extra leash exuded a moldy, old-pee odor. Breathing through her mouth, she attached it to the collar.

She shoved her stockinged toes into the closest pair of flip-flops.

Cramming her phone into the top of the abdomen-splitting hosiery, Peg and her dog, and his leash, and her own leash, raced out.

"Let's go, Nipper. Six twenty-five. I think we can just about make it."

People of all shapes, sizes and accoutrements packed the streets to get to the parade. She held all of the leashes close as they bumped through the crowd.

It was Nipper nirvana. Never in his life had he had the opportunity to walk behind an 80-year-old man wearing only a strategically placed athletic sock.

Or walk next to a woman painted like a GIANT male private part with cotton balls on her face.

Or stop at a crosswalk with AARP's contribution to the Playboy channel.

Parts hung low and loose with easy access for a 50-pound dog.

Peg pushed and shoved her way through the painted sweat. Glitter from strangers' bodies adhered to her skin.

Was that boob glitter? Don't think about it... keep going... can't be late...

She saw a tiny opening in the crowd and urged Nipper in that direction. A drunken pirate staggered up to her, naked from the waist down except for an impressively sized prosthetic penis dangling from his pelvis. At the very end of this swashbuckling schwanz hung a shiny silver hook. He stopped short directly in her path and swayed a bit.

He leaned close to her face with his stenchy, boozy breath. "Wanna dansss doggie syle... ummm... style?" He laughed. "Arrrrr... thassa good wun... get it? Doggie?"

Peg gag-reflexed and backed away. "No, thank you. I'm late for the parade."

He nasty-breathed closer to her. "Oh, c'mon, yur dog likes me." Nipper gnawed at chunks of something crusted on the pirate's boots.

"No, really." Peg turned her face away.

Raising his arms above his head, he ballerina-twirled, round and round he went. His penis hook flew up and gyrated with him. It gained considerable speed and caught on Peg's leash, linking Peg and the pirate in an unwanted pirouette.

"Ahhhh... stop... I have to go."

The pirate stopped moving and put his hands on her shoulders. They both looked down to see his erect hook attached to her.

Peg yelled and jerked herself away and ran as fast as the crowds would let her, Nipper at her heels. Dodging and weaving through the bodies, she slowed when she was sure the pirate was out of sight. She looked down to check on Nipper.

"Nipper, are you all right?" The dog wagged his tail, happily sniffing the pirate's false manhood still firmly connected to her leash.

"Achhhh. Oh my God. Gross." Cringing, she used her thumb and index finger to pluck it off and flick it away. Thudding to the ground, the hook accessory clanged on the concrete. The dog leapt for it and Peg pulled him back.

"Nipper, come on. We're late. Randolph's gonna be so mad. What time is it?" She lifted her snap-flap for her phone.

No phone.

Phone gone.

"Noooooo. Where's my phone?" she wailed. No one noticed. She pounded her hands on her head.

Peg turned in the direction where she thought she had been. But the crowds had grown. She couldn't see past the technicolored skin of the masses. With no concept of her whereabouts, she frantically searched.

Where WERE we? Where ARE we? I can't tell… too confusing…

Creeping along the ground, she saw many disgusting things – but no phone. It was gone. She stood up, gathered her bearings and regrouped.

Okay… phone's gone… horrible… don't freak out… gotta find that float…

A woman wearing a dog collar and leash strode by.

Another dog-float person…

Peg caught hold of her arm. "I'm lost and need to find my friend and his float," Peg yelled over the crowd noise.

"NO INGLÉS," the dog-collared woman yelled back.

"I'm LOST," Peg yelled even louder, then pointed first to the woman's dog collar, then to her own.

The woman smiled and motioned for Peg to follow her.

Peg and Nipper traipsed behind the woman through the teeming rabble. She wound her way in and out of crowded small streets and alleys. The dog-collared woman seemed sure of herself and Peg was not in a position to question.

The parade is over by now… I've no way to contact Randolph.

She and Nipper followed until the woman stopped and pointed to a hotel. The street was packed with costumed, semi-costumed and pretty-much-naked people everywhere. The dog-collared woman turned to face Peg and seemed surprised when she saw Nipper. She shrugged her shoulders then turned away, disappearing into the crowd.

A hotel? Maybe this is where the dog float ended… or started. Where am I?

Nipper led the way into the hotel lobby. The sign said *Fantasy Fest Stations*. A giant man bound with chains attached to his nipples, latex bustier and a studded collar shuffled up to Peg.

"Can I help you?" His booming voice fit his appearance. His chains jingled when he bent down to pet Nipper.

"Yes, please. You see, my husband and I moved here after we sold the business, then he left to help Cuba and I haven't been able to talk to him, and my friend came and got hit on the head with a coconut and life-flighted out and I don't know where she is and my new friend suggested I go on the dog float with him, and I overslept and couldn't find the float... he's gonna be so mad... then a pirate made me dance, and his... well... hook... got caught on me and I lost my phone..."

The large man's mouth gaped.

"So... you see... a woman with a dog collar who didn't speak English," Peg pointed to her own dog collar, "took pity on me and brought me here to find the dog float." She took a breath. "Do you know Randolph, by any chance? Or Lulu, his dog?"

He stared. "Oh. Uh. I'm from Miami. I don't know anyone. I come down on one of the big Fantasy Fest buses. These are the *Fetish* Stations." He continued in a scolding voice, "But no dogs." He looked disgusted.

"The what? The fetish? What are you talking about?"

"Pick one." The humongous man's arm jangled as it pointed to various signs around the room. Nipper licked the giant man's clean-shaven legs through his fishnet stockings, and the man let out a surprisingly high-pitched squeal. "Oooo, that tickles."

Peg pulled on Nipper's leash. Her eyes followed the path of the chained arm: the Dungeon of Dark Secrets, the Kinky Couples, the Den of Desire.

A three-foot-tall man dressed in Daisy Duke jean shorts noticed her looking about and said, "Hey, Dog Lady, you can take *me* for a walk *anytime*." He barked a couple of times and walked away laughing to himself.

Peg's legs weakened and she felt faint. "I gotta get out of here." Yanking Nipper away from the giggling giant, she whirled around. Her snap-flaps flipped in the air. Once out of the door, she realized she had no idea where she was. Who would give her directions? The leprechaun with nipple shamrocks or the pot-smoking flight attendant with "mile high" tattooed on his butt?

She and Nipper dragged themselves through the town until they happened upon a familiar street.

Okay... okay... gonna be okay... no phone... but I can email... I'll apologize with email... as soon as we get home... I'll apologize... again...

They walked under the winking stars, the light breeze hinting of the cooler air to come. Under other conditions, it would have been considered a lovely Caribbean night.

Wasting no time when they got home, Peg opened her laptop to begin her apologies. Instead, she was instantly greeted by an angry email from Randolph.

Email from Randolph

I've left tons of text messages and voice-mails. I held the float for you as long as I could, but since you were a no-show I'm glad I didn't wait any longer. I have no idea what happened to you tonight, but this was a big deal for me and you RUINED it. The Parade Committee is mad at me for delaying the procession. Going against all of my standards, I was forced to allow the sterile French Bulldogs to take the empty spot. It was a total embarrassment. I'm done babysitting you. As far as I'm concerned you are on your own.

The words stung. Peg hovered her fingers over the keyboard to begin her response, paused, then slowly closed the lid.

What's the point? The truth will make him madder. He's right... I'm on my own.

Peg unleashed the collar from her neck and peeled off the remnants of the night. She tossed her clothes in the garbage can. Her big toes throbbed from flip-flopping. Her scalp ached from the pigtail. She turned on the shower, stepped in and knelt on the tile floor. The tiny sparkles of glitter shimmered in the water around the drain. Nipper joined her in the bathroom and glanced at her through the glass shower door.

"How you doin', my only friend?" Peg's voice echoed from the bottom of the shower stall.

He hunched over the rug by the sink, hunkered down – and barfed.

Cuba Crisis

Barking wildly, Nipper dashed down the stairs. Seconds later he was back up again, leaping on and off the bed. When that had no effect, he leapt on and off Peg's stomach as she lay flat on her back under the covers.

"Nipp, it's not even noon yet. Go back to sleep." Peg lifted her foggy head from the pillow. A drool stain covered a large section of the pillowcase. "Nipper, come here." She sat up and patted the bed next to her.

The dog's eyes were crazed. He raced to the front door, his shrill bark increasing in volume and mania. Peg could just make out a knocking sound. "Nipper, it's probably the mailman. It's not that exciting. Please stop barking. Honestly, I think my ears are bleeding."

She covered her ears and sat up in bed, swinging her feet over the side. Her tee shirt crinkled in her stomach creases, turning its embossed photo of Nipper as a puppy into a freakish *Ripley's Believe it or Not* candidate. Walking over to the doorway, she purposely avoided eye contact with her mirrored self. The dog danced on his hind legs, sheep-herding her down the stairs and to the front door.

"Nipper. Calm down. Okay. Okay. I can't answer the door with you leaping all over me." Peg opened the door a tiny crack and peeked out. The dog saw the sliver of light, shoved his pointy nose into the opening, and with one great burst of energy, he barreled out the door and into the arms of the man standing on the front porch.

Peg's muscles jellied.

"Clark?"

"Surprise." Clark crouched on his haunches, while petting and hugging the dog. Nipper overpowered him and Clark fell backward on his butt. "Whoa there, buddy." He pushed Nipper's tongue away from his mouth, "Good to see you too."

Dumbstruck, Peg's mouth gaped. She placed both of her hands on the top of her head in shock. Chunks of glitter tumbled on the ground from her matted hair.

Reality set in. "Oh my God, oh my God." Tears streamed down her face. She dropped to her knees and wrapped her arms around the man-dog melee. Her butt cheeks exposed themselves street-ward in the giant fold-over embrace. A man, a vizsla and a half-naked woman rolled around on the front porch. None of the passersby gave it a second look.

Peg led her husband into the house, "I can't believe you didn't tell me you were coming home. I should be so mad at you but I've had a terrible time of it. Trudy has disappeared, but I think she's all right… I just don't know where she is. Randolph is mad at me because I ruined his dog float at the Fantasy Fest Parade. I hope you get to meet Randolph, but I'm not sure he'll speak to me ever again… so…"

Clark put his finger to her lips. "First of all," he nuzzled her neck, "before we do any more talking," he nibbled her earlobe, "why don't we see if that tiny Key West shower," he lifted her shirt, "fits two people."

I better brush my teeth.

"I'll go make us some coffee." In an agile move, Clark jumped out of bed and into his briefs. He turned his head sideways to catch a glimpse of his six-pack abs in the dresser mirror.

"Coffee in the late afternoon? So sinful." She admired the sight of her husband in his tight-fitting briefs. "I like your undies. I thought it was hard to get new clothing in Cuba." Peg leaned across the bed and snapped the waistband of his tighty-whities as he picked up his khaki shorts from the floor.

He bent down and kissed her. "Just like the rum and sugar – all government issued." Leaving the room he said, "You stay up here and relax. It's still with cream and sugar, right?"

"We call it con leche and azucar here," Peg called after him as he descended the stairs.

Peg leisurely got out of bed and walked into the bathroom. She was glad that she'd had the wherewithal to do a thorough bathroom clean-up last night. She tied her hair into a stylish knot, applied skin cream, face powder and a light lipstick. Slipping into a Chinese silk bathrobe, she admired the pale pink color against her skin. She tied the belt loosely around her waist.

Clark was sitting at the kitchen counter staring at his computer screen. He closed the lid. "Your coffee, senorita." He handed her a steaming cup.

Peg took a careful sip then set the cup down. Settling into Clark's lap, she picked some glitter off his arm. "I'm glad you're back. I'm sorry for being such a pest. The lack of communication and the heat and the newness of everything... well... just got to me." Her eyes welled up.

Clark smiled a swarthy grin and stroked her thigh under her bathrobe. "I have a gift for you." He handed her a small painted wooden box. "This was carved by a local Cuban craftsman."

"Oh, Clark, it's lovely." She traced the engraved heart shape on the top of the box with her finger. "I love all of the little drawers and compartments... very intricate."

"When I saw it, I thought of you – beautiful and–" He hesitated.

"Lots of room for storage?" Peg laughed and patted her mid-section.

"No – perfectly constructed." He kissed her.

"I have so much to tell you. I'm so worried about Trudy–"

Clark's phone buzzed. The screen said *unknown number*. He sideways-glanced, but ignored it.

The dog barked at a lizard outside the back door window. Clark shifted Peg off of his lap and walked over to open the door. Nipper kangaroo-hopped onto the deck onto the unsuspecting reptile.

Clark laughed at a long green tail sticking out of the dog's mouth. "He's a good hunter now. And speaking of food, I'm starving. Let's go get something to eat."

Peg shrieked, "Nipper, no." She ran to the dog and pried open his mouth, allowing the lizard to drop to the ground and slither between the deck planks. "There are so many poisonous things here. We already had one horrible incident with a giant frog from HELL... it was–"

Clark cut her off. "I could eat a giant frog right about now." He pulled a shirt over his head. "You go get dressed, and we'll walk to Salute on the Beach. I love their yellowtail snapper."

"Umm, right. Good." Peg leaned over Nipper, looking into his mouth. "Are you hiding anything that I should know about?"

The dog wagged his tail innocently.

Clark put his phone in his pocket.

The Atlantic Ocean sucked some of the air's humidity back into the water. The breeze was calm. The margaritas were pale, green and cold.

"Coffee and a margarita... perfect start to the day's diet." Peg held up her glass. "Cheers."

Clark cheersed then chugged his beverage. He waved at the waiter to bring two more.

"Okay. Wow." Peg wide-eyed the green glasses lined up on the table. "I should eat a piece of bread or something." She picked up a warm slice from the basket. "Is everything all right? I mean, with us?"

"Yes. Yes, most definitely." Clark clasped her hand across the table. "We're stronger than ever because we're a team. I mean, look at us – we buy and sell companies together."

Peg inhaled and took a big swig of her drink. "Okaaay."

"You are my favorite CFO and the smartest woman I know. I couldn't have done any of the finances without you." Clark stared, unblinking.

Peg half-laughed, "I *guess* that's a good thing. I'd kinda rather hear that you think I'm beautiful and that you love me more than anything in the world."

"Of course you are and of course I do." Clark kissed the top of her hand and then patted it. "But your financial savvy is what has allowed us to have the life we live today – in the place where we live." He motioned around the restaurant's open-air room toward the ocean.

"Well, it's the place that *I live…* by myself. So I'm thinking that I wish I was worse with numbers."

"I'll return soon – to stay. I promise. But I have a request for you. I'd like to go back to our buyer and accept the lump sum distribution from the sale of the company. They said that we could renegotiate those terms if we wanted to – that it would always be an option. I think it's a good idea." Clark squeezed her hand.

"What? Why would we do that? We make considerably more money over time with the ten-year distribution. Why would we cut our noses off like that?" Peg moved her hand.

"We used the first distribution to buy the house." Clark covered her hand with his.

Peg countered, "*Your* idea to buy the house."

"*Your* idea to pay cash." Clark's jaw tensed.

"Yes, because I hate mortgage payments," Peg hissed back.

Clark's voice calmed. "But now we have less to live on. And we don't *have to have* less to live on if we do the lump sum payment." Clark released her hands to grab more drinks from the waiter.

"We'd have *plenty* to live on if you'd get paid real money on your project and stopped cashing checks from our account every week." Peg clasped her hands in her lap.

Clark held his hands up surrender-style. "Right, I know, I know. Forget about what I just said. What I mean is I think that we should use the lump sum payout to buy a business in Key West. You pick the investment. You always make the right decisions. You can name it Peg's Company." Clark scooted his chair next to hers.

"Really. We just sold a business."

"Yes, and look how well we did – we have a learning curve going."

"Umm, I'll have to think about it." Tilting her head, she watched a rooster chase two chickens around the orchid garden next to the restaurant gate. "I do miss running a company." She threw a piece of bread towards the rooster to give the chickens a chance to escape. "Maybe a business with no overheads and minimal investment."

"Yes. Sure. Whatever you want. Our money will make money and you'll have a project of your own." Clark looked hopeful.

Both Savages drank.

Clark leaned his head close to hers. "You think about it. We can talk at the house after dinner."

The booze was having an impact. Her head wobbled. "Okay, I guess so, I mean… I still don't know."

And she didn't.

When Peg woke up the next day, her lips felt like dried-up sea sponges sealed together to contain dead sea creatures in her mouth.

Did I smoke cigarettes last night?

Nipper licked her fingertips that dangled off the bed. The other side of the bed was empty except for a note from Clark.

Peg, I'll be back. Thanks for signing the agreement, Love Clark

Right, dim memory. He's gone and I signed another drunk agreement.

When she sat up in bed, her stomach contents stubbornly refused to sit up with her. She gingerly placed her head back on the pillow. Wiping the fuzz from her eyes, she saw the folder labeled *Alternate Contract for Sale of Company* on the nightstand. She leaned on her elbow to move the empty shot glasses from the top of the folder. The glasses clinked and the strong smell of left-over tequila triggered a gag. Holding the file over her head, she shook it.

Empty

Without a phone, she checked her computer for emails – no messages.

Too hung over to care as much as she otherwise would have, she got up, let out the dog, fed the dog and went back to bed. Nipper curled up at her feet. When night-time crept into the room, she forced herself awake. Stumbling into the kitchen, she prayed that some do-gooder had made her a double cheeseburger with bacon and left it on the counter.

"So I should be happy now, right Nipper?" The dog sat at attention. "I mean, he came home and promised that he'll be back again soon. Like he said, it's all good."

A blast of cold air swirled around her legs. She shivered and wrapped her robe tightly around her.

A green aura appeared on the kitchen counter. The shape of a six-toed cat hovered over the carved wooden box on the counter. Snow White's tail flicked menacingly. The lights dimmed.

"Oh no you don't. That's from Clark. It proves he loves me." Peg lunged for the gift, but she was too slow. The cat's tail swished the box off of the counter and sent it flying into the wall with such force that the wood smashed into pieces.

Peg ran to the broken bits on the floor. "No. Why did you do that?"

The haintly feline sauntered in midair. With her dextrous six-toed front paw, the cat opened the kitchen desk drawer, levitated a folder labeled *Emergency Cash and Traveler's Checks* and zoomed the file across the room, where it came to a rest next to an incredulous Peg.

"You beast," Peg screamed.

The translucent cat raised her back leg, licked her private parts and disappeared.

Peg scrambled to find the pieces of the box. She located one of the tiny compartments with a hidden piece of paper wedged in the slats. Her heart leapt. A secret love note – from Clark.

It read:

Clark, my love, I can't wait until we can be together forever. Todo mi amor – BENITA.

... not possible...

Peg read the note again.

... a re-gift from his mistress... to HIM...

... the box wasn't for me... he lied...

Nipper took interest in the manilla folder next to her. He sniffed and pawed the label on the cover. Peg tug-of-warred the file away from the dog, but when she opened it up, it too was empty. The cash was gone. The traveler's checks were gone. She slumped against the wall.

A militaristic masculine voice echoed through the house: "Get up woman – and fight like a man. He's after your money."

A southern drawl oozed from the vents: "You should know all about that, Ernie."

"Shut up you miserable excuse for a writer," Hemingway bellowed.

Why? Why is he doing this to me? What about love? What about a new company together... lump sum payout?

"Sugar, he's just playin' you. One lump or two – doesn't matter – he's biding his time 'til he takes you for everything," Tennessee snarked.

Peg collapsed into the fetal position.

There's nothing left to take.

Drinkin' It All In

Empty liquor bottles toppled as Peg reached for the chili cheese Fritos on the coffee table. Leaning across her dog, she dug her orange-stained fingers into the bag and cupped a handful of chips.

"One fur you."

Nipper gently lipped the chip from her grasp.

"Two... okay." She waved her hand in front of her face, shaking her wobbly head. "More than two fur me. Ha ha." She gobbled a mouthful of chips. She wiped her carrot-colored palm on her flannel pajamas, the armpits stiff with three-day-old sweat. Her pajama pants billowed jodphur-like out of her knee-length Italian leather boots.

The channel changer's buttons were caked with grimy crud, making them no longer functional. The homebuying channel remained on the screen day and night, with no rest for the world-wide homebuyers. The couple in the Caribbean held hands as they decided on what house to buy on their island paradise. Peg shouted at the TV, "Don't do it. Oh shhhure, he promissses you aventure... HATE THAT WORD... take it from me, girlfriend, he'll leave you alone... by yurself... oh... an watch the coconuttts too... not kiddinabout that." She waggled her pointer finger at the screen.

The doorbell rang. Peg stumbled to answer it. The mail-lady stepped back when she saw Peg. "Hello, Mrs. Savage. You're still here? There's a tropical depression, you know." She handed Peg a stack of mail.

"Than' you very much, donn you worry... I've alllreddddy got it." Peg closed the door and re-stumbled back to the couch.

Holding Nipper's head, she pressed her nose against his face. "Randolph is shhhuper mad, I should shheck emails, but I'm not gunna. He's done with me. I got only you now... no husband... no Trudy... juss ma dog." A drunk tear trickled down her cheek and landed on Nipper's paws. The dog, drawn in by the proximity of her foul breath, licked her cheesy lips. Peg hugged him close. Her head fell to the couch armrest and she passed out.

Had she not been trashed for three days she would have noticed:

Day one: the weather warnings on all of the other TV channels, the wind picking up, the barometric pressure dropping

Day two: the pounding rain, the tropical depression

Day three: the tropical-depression-turned-hurricane's unexpected turn toward the Florida Keys, the power outage, and–

A humongous hunk of blue paint missing from the front porch ceiling.

From the darkness of inebriated sleep, her eyelids opened to a vision of unblinking dog eyeballs, eerily reflecting the electrifying lightning flashes. A huge crash of thunder bolted her upright. "Ahhh, oh my God, oh my God, oh my God." Her tongue was a cotton ball wrapped in a dirty sweater.

The rain pelted the windows and the shutters banged against the siding. The roar was deafening like a–

Freight train… it sounds like a freight train… that's how you'll know it's a…

"HURRICANE." She leapt off the couch. "Nipper, come." Instantly sobered by fear, she corralled the dog into the bedroom and shut the door.

All my fault… the grotto… so sorry Sister Gabriel…

Why didn't I follow the hurricane readiness checklist? I'm not ready… no phone… I didn't get bottled water… or a seven-day supply of non-perishable food… or batteries… or plastic plates…

She opened the nightstand drawer and found a tiny reading flashlight, formerly used so she wouldn't wake up Clark.

Clark, you son of a bi–

CRASH. The windows rattled and a picture fell from its hook.

Peg clutched her chest. "Nipper, on the bed!" She knelt on the floor and felt around for the doggie life jacket that Clark had bought to take Nipper out on boating excursions.

"I should have been suspicious when he didn't buy *me* a life jacket. At least *one* of us is going to survive this." She crawled on top of the bed and kissed Nipper on the head, shakily slipping the blue vest around the dog's body and fastening the straps.

Something heavy careened into the back of the house. The sound of shattering glass filled the air.

"Ayyyy, what was that?"

She hustled Nipper under the covers. The top of her head made a tent with the sheets. The torrential rain pounded the metal roof. The walls creaked and moaned.

Life passed before her. She thought about her mom and Gram – how much they had meant to her – how much she had loved them. How she wished they were here with her now.

Their jewelry… I have to save their jewelry.

Throwing off the blankets, she crept across the mattress to the dresser. Another resounding crash and the house quaked. She scampered under the covers, clutching her jewelry box. A trickle of water formed under the bedroom door.

"This is what it's come to, Nipper. You'll be my treasure ship." Peg dumped the jewelry on the bed, holding the flashlight between her chin and neck. She fondled the family heirloom bracelet, worn by every baby girl for 100 years. She clasped it onto Nipper's collar. The tiny stream of light shone on an engraved heart locket, given to her by her mother. Peg picked it up. It read, *To Peg, my little ray of sunshine.*

I could use a little ray of sunshine right about now…

Peg pinned the locket to the outside of Nipper's life jacket. "There… like a purple heart for bravery." Nipper's brow formed a wrinkly upside down V over his dark brown eyes. Peg scratched his ear.

Her grandmother's gold and silver necklaces turned Nipper into the canine version of King Tut. "I don't want to weigh you down, my good friend. The rest'll be on me." Peg stifled a sob. "The sunken treasure." Nipper sat on the bed like an Egyptian sphinx, solemnly taking on his responsibility.

Peg squashed rings on her fingers and loaded bracelets on her wrists. She moved her arms robotically, watching the reflection of the jewels glint under the makeshift tent. The emerald earrings that Clark had given her caught her eye.

Back when he cared…

She looked down at her pajama shirt. Lifting her right breast, she picked off an orange-colored chip-goo-ball and replaced it with the green and gold earrings. "You'll be safe under there… one day you'll be discovered," she cooed as she patted her breast down. The earrings disappeared in the shirt, under the wine-stained words, *I love my bed.*

Peg and Nipper jingled together in their huddle. The little flashlight's battery grew dim.

The room darkened and the gale forces howled. The rain intensified in waves – thunderous, then backing off.

Out of nowhere, Nipper sat erect and cocked his head. He turned frantic, leaping back and forth under the tent, then jumped off the bed.

"Nipper, what's the matter? What is it?" Peg un-tented herself in the unlit room.

Nipper body-slammed into the door, barking furiously. Peg hurried off of the bed to get to the berserk animal. The dog hopped back and forth, madly gyrating his head as Peg clasped her ringed fingers around the knob. Thinking she would peek through a crack in the door, she inched it open. Nipper had another thought – he wedged his nose into the small opening, forced the door wide open and bolted.

"Nipper, come here. It's dangerous." Peg followed his craziness down the hallway, where he resumed his frenetic behavior. He bounded into the front door, leaving claw marks as he fell to the floor.

"Nipper, you'll hurt yourself." Peg wrenched him back, only to have him wriggle away from her.

In an instant, all hell broke loose. The front door opened with a huge blast of wind and rain. Seizing his opportunity, Nipper darted out onto the porch. He stopped briefly, crouched into an athletic pre-launch pose, then leapt into the river of water that once was the street. Peg yelled for him but all she could see was his neck bling and shiny metal heart, swimming away.

"Nipper. Nipper," she screamed, delirious.

The pelting rain forced her to clamp her eyes shut. She clutched the porch column to steady herself against the wind.

How am I gonna get him? How can I do this? Too much water...

When she opened her eyes, she noticed a green glowing mist on the bottom stoop. A mini waterspout formed and images took shape. Two ghostly Key West writers and a polydactyl cat lounged comfortably on the step.

Furious and frustrated at the impossibility of her situation, Peg lashed out. "Oh, so are you here to torture me again? To see me suffer? That's what you want? You guys are really assholes. Maybe if you did something worthwhile you wouldn't be the *un*dead. Maybe you would be just *regular* dead... maybe you could move on, or whatever it is that spirits are supposed to do. WHY don't you help me, you useless asshole haints?" Peg punched the rain in their direction.

Hemingway and Williams calmly nodded to each other and stood up. Snow White wound herself around their legs. The men linked arms and formed a shield in front of Peg. Snow White floated off and glowed brightly over the runaway dog, who swam with the current, on a mission.

Distracted, Peg strained her eyes in the direction of the light, cupping her hand over her eyebrows. "Nipper, I can see you."

The ghost shield lit up the street. Hemingway pointed to a paddleboard that was wedged perpendicular to a large concrete street light down the street. Water cascaded around the sides of the board forming a raging current.

"What? A paddleboard? Hell nooo. You're crazy. I'll die for sure," she yelled at the haints.

They shoulder-shrugged.

"I'm not a good swimmer."

They nodded, unabashed.

Before she could respond, the luminescent figures appeared behind her. Smirking to each other, they lifted their radiant right feet in unison, and swiftly kicked her hindquarters – into the ocean-slash-river-slash-street.

She sputtered and gasped for air after she hit the water. Her body tossed and rolled in the current that surged higher and lower. Taking a breath, she realized she could touch the bottom. Her Italian leather boots protected her feet from the random sharp objects. She tippytoe-swam her way toward the paddleboard. A greenish glow surrounded her in the wind and the rain as she careened down the street. Chunks of palm trees and roof tiles blew past, but miraculously, not into her.

Please, no dead bodies floating by… please God… no dead bodies.

She tossed and turned, gasping in the current until she bonked into the board with considerable force. Peg managed to grab hold of the board's strap and secure it to her wrist. Swim-walking into the turbulent street she used the force of the water and her body to wrench the board off the street light. The paddleboard flung into the air like a rocket and jetted past her in the rapids, forcing her underwater. It dragged her up and down like a fish flailing on the line.

I'm sorry to all the fish in the world… for mocking your suffering… this is horrible.

The board twirled several times, swirling her in a circle, before straightening out and gaining speed. Peg had just enough time to grab the end of it. She hoisted her body onto the board before it crashed into a parked truck and began to spin again.

Throughout the twists and turns she could see Nipper and the glowing, green ball hovering above him. "Nipper, I'm coming."

Supernatural strength helped her heave her entire self to a prone position on the board. In alligator fashion, Peg scooped her ringed fingers into the shape of oars and dug into the passing water. A plastic pink flamingo projectiled past her cheek. A beach umbrella missile launched in her direction, only to open up and tornado into the sky when it got close. A shoe, towel, coffee cup and lamp spun in a furious dance, then hastily changed course.

My God, it's like a rummage sale in hell.

An unnatural phosphorescence oozed around her.

Even though Nipper swam with incredible speed, her paddle-board drew near. Through the din of the storm, Peg heard a familiar bark.

Lulu?

He's going for Lulu... she's in that stranded trolley bus.

Nipper swam into the trolley from one of the open windows on the side, but the rough water forced him toward the front of the trolley. Head down, shoulders tensed, he thrashed his front legs against the strong tides.

Lulu perched precariously on the top of a fire extinguisher case at the back of the flooded bus. The water whirlpooled, swelling in and out of the opening below her. She howled when she saw Nipper, stopping to snarl at the odd piece of rubbish flying by.

"I'm coming, Nipper. I'm coming, Lulu." Peg crashed the paddleboard into the rear of the trolley. She maneuvered it sideways to force it into the trolley's rear window. Once through, the board caught the angry current and it blasted past the stranded chihuahua, straight into the front windshield.

The force of the hit tossed Peg off of the board. The water roiled and whorled around her. She held fast to the board, the antique grooves in her many rings providing a good grip. The water alternately lifted then submerged her body as she battled to stay close to the board. She contorted her neck in the water to gain a visual of Nipper on the driver's side at the front of the bus. The water level ebbed and flowed angrily. She could see him tiring. Against his effort, he drifted sideways toward the turbulent maelstrom outside of the trolley's front window. It sucked Nipper closer and closer.

"Nipper, watch out," Peg shrieked.

The raging vortex caught his back leg and dragged him down.

"Nipper, noooooo."

Peg released her death clutch on the paddleboard. A deluge of water catapulted her body toward the steering wheel. She smashed into the windshield feet first, and, in one Herculean move, swung her Italian leather boots to either side of the driver's door. Using the adrenaline of a mother lifting a Volkswagen off of her baby, she caught the silver and gold chains rotating around the dog's neck and hauled the exhausted dog out of the maelström. Gripping the top of Nipper's life vest, she propelled herself backward. The muddy water splashed over her head, obstructing her vision, but she gritted her teeth and lunged for the wedged paddleboard. She caught hold, choking to keep her head above the churning water. A freakish wave lifted the duo and they both landed on top of the board.

Necklaces... thank you, Grams...

Peg and Nipper's bodies strained to stabilize on the undulating paddleboard surface. She turned to Lulu.

"Lulu, I'm here," Peg screamed from the front of the bus. Lulu's back leg dangled crookedly at the little dog's side. "Oh, Lulu, your leg." Lulu barked and whined – her beady black eyes bulged with fear. The water raged at the little dog's feet, lapping at the fire extinguisher case, which loosened with the strain.

Peg surveyed the situation. The current was too strong for her to get to Lulu. Lulu must come to Peg.

Quickly unfastening one of Nipper's life jacket straps, she wrapped it around the trolley's rearview mirror – in case he fell off of the board. She un-wristed the board strap and tied it to the mirror, not wanting the paddleboard to twist away with her attached to it. Confident that both Nipper and the board were secured, Peg now had one hand for stability and the other hand to deal with Lulu.

Please God, let this be a strong mirror.

Peg yelled toward the back of the bus, "Lulu, you need to jump. I'll catch you."

Lulu whined. Her hind leg drooped.

"I know it's scary, but you can do it, Lulu. Jump! I'm here." Peg held up a hand for encouragement.

The little dog cried.

"Lulu, please jump."

The chihuahua cowered.

"I will catch you." Peg waved her blingy hand. "Please." Before Peg could finish her plea, a glowing cat appeared behind the small dog. With a big yawn, the feline apparition dramatically separated two large claws from an outstretched paw. A quick flick of the sharp talons, and the chihuahua sailed into the water. The leap surprised Peg as much as Lulu. The little dog sank swiftly, only to reappear briefly in the rapids and sink again. Peg slid from the board and dove under the water. In the haze of agitated dirt and gunk, a shadow drifted by. Peg gasped to the surface, holding Lulu by the tail.

They slammed into the windshield.

Lulu sputtered and shook. Pushing herself off of the windshield against the wall of water, Peg grasped the board while cradling the scared pup. Peg pushed Lulu up on the board next to Nipper. She attached Lulu's collar to Nipper's life vest. Nipper whined and nudged the tiny dog with his head.

"Good girl."

"Good boy."

Peg re-hoisted herself onto the board. The water level in the trolley rose precariously high. Worried they would get crushed, Peg huddled on hands and knees over the dogs in a protective stance. The board continued to rise and fall with the surge. Peg lifted her butt higher into an upside down V until it touched the ceiling…

…Bump…

…Bump…

…Bump…

… until all that was saving them from a watery grave was her sheltering down-dog pose.

Even in my compromised state, I get the irony…

From cat pose, to cow pose to down dog, the trio rose and fell with the tidal flow.

Lulu shielded by Nipper.

Nipper shielded by Peg.

All three shielded by a green fog surrounding the trolley.

Apology Accepted

The wind died. The rain stopped. The small police boat maneuvered down the street in the dark. Piles of floating debris littered the path.

Nipper barked.

"Nipper, what is it?" Peg's waterlogged brain gained awareness. "Oh my God, it's a boat!"

"In here. We're in here," she yelled from the shadows. The boat's spotlight moved in the direction of the flooded trolley.

"Here... in the front." Peg shook her head to get their attention, not wanting to un-huddle the dogs.

The boat cut the engine and navigated closer.

"Are you okay?" a man called into the trolley from the boat. "How many are you?"

The dogs started to bark. Peg answered. "It's me, Peg Savage, and two dogs. Help us."

"We'll need a life raft and some life jackets," the man ordered his boat partner.

"Are you Peg Savage the finance tutor?"

"Ummm. Yes, that's me."

"Thanks for helping Tom pass his class. I'm his dad."

"Ehhh... you're welcome. Does that mean that you'll save us now?" Peg pleaded.

"Is one of the dogs a chihuahua, by any chance? We're on a special lookout for a white chihuahua."

"Yes. I have a vizsla and a chihuahua with me."

"Hang tight, we have a rescue boat on its way."

"What? Don't leave us," Peg yelled over the noise of the barking dogs.

"The larger boat is on its way. Hang tight. We need to move forward. Searching for victims. Assessing. Rescue comes after us." The engines started and they moved out into the black water.

Peg's hope sank but she quieted the dogs. "It's okay. Someone else is coming... I think I hear another boat."

Another engine sound reverberated toward them. The larger Fish and Wildlife boat approached and a man secured it to the trolley. The immense spotlight blinded Peg. The dogs barked crazily.

"Peg? Is that you, Peg? And Nipper and Lulu." Bernie's voice broke when he saw them. "Oh, Lulu, we've been looking everywhere for you. Randolph, look."

Peg screamed in the direction of the boat. "Yes. It's us... all of us."

Randolph wept. "Oh, Lulu. We were so worried. How did you get out, you little she-devil?"

"Get the life raft." The captain issued orders and Bernie stepped into the miniature blow-up raft. He paddled it into the trolley and next to the stranded group.

"Oh, thank God you found us." Peg handed over Lulu. "She's injured. Her back leg's broken."

Bernie tenderly cradled the trembling dog. He nestled her inside his own jacket and wiped away a tear, looking back to see if anyone from the FWC noticed.

He reached for Nipper. Peg unfastened the dog's life jacket straps from the mirror. The large dog landed with a plop in the middle of the raft.

"There you are, Big Boy," Bernie settled the dog.

Peg winced in pain when Bernie steadied her waist and lifted her off of the paddleboard into the boat. The heirloom rings hung loose on her pruney fingers. Her knees and elbows throbbed from the night's exertion. Bernie's strong, gentle arms placed her next to him on the raft. The three of them folded into his embrace.

Bernie guided the raft to the side of the rescue boat. He lovingly withdrew the tiny wounded dog from his jacket and lightly placed her in Randolph's outstretched arms. Randolph sobbed. "Lulu, our baby. We were so worried. You poor, poor adorable beast."

Bernie lifted Nipper into the boat. The big dog gravitated toward Lulu. He licked Randolph's salty face.

"Randolph, put Lulu in the basket. Swaddle her in the blankets.

I knew we would find her. And we did thanks to Peg." Bernie's voice broke again. Randolph carefully covered Lulu with a polka-dotted blanket and gingerly placed her into a sparkly bassinet on the boat floor. Nipper kept a close watch, his head resting on the basket's edge.

Randolph grabbed Peg's arm to help her up the ladder. Once in the boat, he held Peg in a giant bear hug and squeezed her tightly. He spoke earnestly in her ear. "I'm sorry. I shouldn't have treated you that way. I know you have an explanation, albeit a ridiculous one, about why you didn't make the parade."

Peg pulled herself back to catch her breath. "The truth is that I got entangled by a pirate penis, and then followed a dog-collared woman to a fetish hotel, where I was propositioned by a midg... ehhh... dwar... umm... smaller-than-average man, who wore Daisy Duke shorts."

Randolph nestled his cheek close to hers. "I apologize again, that doesn't sound ridiculous at all." He re-squeezed her. "We'll never mention it – water under the bridge. I have no idea how you saved my dog tonight, but I thank you from the bottom of my cold heart. I hope that you can accept *all of my* apologies."

"Of course I do. You're my friend. And this is a friendly island. That's what we do here. Or so I've heard." She smiled.

He grinned and looked at her, "Thank y–" He stopped, his eyed widened. "Oh my, honey, you look atrocious, I mean really – awful. Like, Sasquatchy bad... except for your jewelry," he glanced down at her feet, "and your Italian leather boots. A bit overdone though."

Her skin puckered everywhere around the newly forming bruises. Randolph covered Peg's shoulders with a towel and sat with her on the boat bench. Hesitating, he reached in his pocket and took out a rubber band. He whispered, "I'm gonna put your hair up in this, doll. Just take my word on it." He pulled her wet hair into a ponytail and tamped down the flyaways.

"They're waterproof." Peg eyes were half closed.

"What are, sweetie?"

"The Italian leather boots... they're waterproof."

"Ahhh. Well done then."

Randolph draped his arm around her. She leaned on him.

Bernie loaded the life raft into the boat. "Peg, you and Nipper are coming home with us. We'll sort out your house in the daylight. I'm sure it took a beating."

The captain started the engines. The searchlight scanned from left to right as they backed away. Through bleary eyes, Peg noticed the sign on the side of the trolley that had saved them from the storm – GHOST TOUR.

... *not doomed*...

Assholio

Peg saw the *request to chat* blinking on her computer screen. She hesitated, then pushed the accept button.

Clark's face appeared on the screen, "Peg, are you okay? I've been so worried about you. What about Nipper?"

Peg stared deadpan into his face. "Other than almost dying, we're fine." Her eyes narrowed.

"Oh, thank God."

Peg's voice was measured. "Cut the bullshit, Clark. I know about Benita. I found the note… in the beautiful gift that she gave you. "

"Peg, I can–"

Peg cut him off. "You can't drink me into believing you any-more… and definitely not from Cuba."

"But nothing's happened, I promise."

"This is all for *her*. You're doing this for *her*." Peg's voice wavered then steadied. "Just admit it – for once – tell the truth."

Clark twisted his strained neck and looked away from the screen.

Peg was quiet.

Clark filled the silence. "I got notification that the lump sum payment came through."

"Yes. It did."

"I don't see any money in the account."

"I know. I moved it."

The vein in Clark's forehead bulged. "You moved it? Where?"

"I put it somewhere safe."

"*All* of it?" His face darkened.

"Yes." Peg stared unblinking at the computer. "And I changed banks and bank accounts."

"What? You can't do that without me." Clark raged and pointed at the screen.

"Yes, I can… and I did." Peg's voice was unruffled.

Clark growled. "How am I going to live?"

Peg gazed past the computer and out of the window at Pierre who was piling up the massive fallen branches in the yard. "I hear that the Cuban government gives a monthly stipend of twenty-five dollars. You might want to make a budget spreadsheet."

"You bitch. I didn't even screw this one – yet."

Peg clicked off the computer.

Her phone buzzed into voicemail. Her emails dinged unopened. Her texts lit up – ignored.

She put on her work gloves and ripped open a box of large black garbage bags.

Time to clean up this mess.

Gift to the Sea

Peg watched the crabs dart up and down the algae-covered rocks at the end of the pier. "It's amazing how clean the ocean looks, considering what it's just been through."

Randolph held an emerald heart earring up to his ear and snapped a selfie. "Does it have to be the emeralds? Why can't it be the pearls? You know – back to their homeland?"

Peg grabbed the earring from him. "It's gotta be the emeralds. No substitution. These were Clark's bribe to get me to move. Dirty money."

"But why?"

"He must have brought me here because financials are a lot more attractive to get divorced in Florida than Illinois. In Florida there's no need to predict future tax liability. We had to have residency here for six months before he could file…"

Randolph's eyes glazed over.

Peg continued, "Anyway, believe me, it's obvious." Reaching into her pocket, she took out the newspaper picture. "And, because of her. He wants HER." With three fingers wrapped tightly around the emeralds, she jabbed her finger at Clark and the mystery woman.

Randolph took a better look at the picture. "You mean HIM?"

"Yes – of course, *Clark*. I'm talking about HER – the woman next to Clark." Peg pointed to the dark-haired beauty.

"Doll, that's a HIM underneath all that HER. That's Benita, the famous Cuban drag queen. Been trying for ages to get an American sugar daddy to marry, you know – to become a citizen."

"What? No, that's his *translator*."

"You got the *trans* part right." Randolph sideways-eye-rolled.

"You've got to be kidding me."

"No. 'Fraid not."

"Really?"

"'Fraid so."

Silence.

Tipping his head toward Peg, Randolph whispered, "He's expecting Beauty. He's going to have *quite* a surprise when The Beast shows up." Randolph thought for a moment. "Like dating Beyonce but being carried over the threshold by Jay Z." He paused. "Caitlin comes to dinner but Bruce goes to—"

"I get it. Stop." Peg plugged her ears.

Randolph stood up straight. "Right, sorry." He motioned a lip-zip.

Peg grasped Randolph's hand and turned it palm up. "Here." She firmly pressed the emeralds into his hand.

"Really?" The heart earrings glinted in the sun.

"Yeah."

Randolph put his arm around her shoulders. "Margaret." Peg gave him a quizzical look. "I feel like this is a time for formality, and, *Margaret* is such a regal name." He cleared his throat, "He really is a *terrible* person for doing this to you."

Silence

Peg stared at the blue horizon. "A real conch-sucker."

Bridging the Fear

On a hot, sunny day in Key West, Peg put on her polarized, fog-free, designer sunglasses. "I'm *not* sure this is a good idea." Her heartbeat quickened. Her clammy hands slid down the steering wheel into her lap. She slouched in the driver's seat and gave Randolph a pleading look.

Randolph's emerald earring twinkled. "You can do it, doll. Oh, and BTW your manicure looks FABULOUS."

Peg sat up straight. "I know. I *love* the color. See my toes too?" Peg wiggled her toes in her sandals.

"Chills down my spine." He spoke like a proud parent. "Speaking of good looking–" He slid his Ray-Bans down his nose and peered at Peg over the top of the glasses. "Pierre wishes you luck on your endeavor today."

"Pierre does?" Peg cursed her blood that pinked involuntarily under her transparent skin. "When did you talk to him?"

"He invited Bernie and me to go fishing with him on that gorgeous boat."

"Oh. He knows Bernie too?"

"He does now. You kinda did us a favor. Bernie got to know him at the FWC office after the – well – you know. The *other* event that we don't speak about."

"You're welcome," Peg snipped.

Randolph checked on Lulu and Nipper who were sitting up in the back seat of Peg's car. Lulu's pink cast matched the bows on her ears. "I wonder if I should have gotten them life jackets."

"Forget it. I can't do it." Peg lifted the door handle and bailed out of the driver's side of the car.

Randolph draped himself over the empty driver's seat. "I'm just kidding. A joke. You're going to be fine. Now get back in here."

Peg's phone rang with a video call. Randolph handed her the phone and Peg swiped the screen to answer, "Hi, how's today?"

Trudy's face appeared on the screen. "Hey. I'm good. I thought this was the big day. Why are you standing *outside* of the car?"

"Because she's a ninny, that's why," Randolph called through the open door. "Now get in the car, Peg."

Trudy's voice got bossy on the phone, "Listen, Peg, if *I* can survive an unconscious ride in a helicopter AND waking up in *God-knows-where USA,* you can do this. I mean, privacy laws my ass, they wouldn't even tell *me* where I was." She was getting worked up.

Peg got in the car and closed the door. "I know... we talked about this already. You told me to tell you when we've talked about things before – right?"

Trudy said, "We did? Oh, okay. The great thing about concussions is that every day is a new day. I mean *brand new.*" She removed her glasses and rubbed her temples. "However, I *did* remember that this is the big day for you, so let's get going."

Peg propped up the phone on the dashboard and started the car. She sighed. "Clark always did the driving."

The image of Trudy's mouth filled the phone screen: "The asshole isn't there. You have to do it yourself."

"I know. I know. I'm gonna do it," Peg shrieked.

Trudy backed down. Her voice calmed. "Okay then. Randolph, is she ready?"

"She's as ready as she'll *ever* be."

Peg gave him the eye.

He added, "I mean *yes,* she's ready."

"Nipper and Lulu, is she ready?" Trudy asked in a high-pitched dog-owner voice.

"They didn't answer. Can they hear me?"

Randolph jumped in, "Yes, Trudy, they can hear you. They're not used to talking in a video chat. They think she's ready."

"Keep breathing, sweetie." Randolph looked at Peg's blood-drained face.

"Don't overthink it, Peg." Trudy spoke through hands held in prayer over her lips.

Peg put the car in drive, signaled, then turned right onto US1.

I can do this… I can do this… I can do this.

She accelerated to the fully allowable 35 miles per hour, drove for five seconds, and –

"I made it." Peg exhaled.

"Peg – you did it." Trudy's face whooped and hollered on the phone screen.

Peg turned the car into an empty lot and parked. One by one, she un-suctioned her fingers from the steering wheel.

Randolph made the sign of the cross and laughed. He reached over and gave Peg a big hug. "Congratulations, Cow Key Bridge – 300 feet of terror."

"I really did it." Peg raised her fists in victory.

"Only 41 more to go!"

The End

Acknowledgments

Dear Reader,

Peg, the protagonist in *Island Life Sentence*, faces a hurricane in Key West, Florida.

I'm writing these acknowledgments in my third evacuation location while fleeing the path of Hurricane Irma. The irony of this situation does not escape me. The odd thing is – I feel fortunate. The eye of the hurricane missed our island and our house. There are so many people in the Keys that can't say that. My heart goes out to them.

When packing to evacuate my house, it was surreal to have to choose which items I wanted to save. To look around the rooms and make decisions – do I keep the pictures my kids made for me when they were little? What about my Italian leather boots? Nope. They won't fit. We were instructed to take a two-week supply of food and water – not to mention flashlights, batteries and poop bags for the dog and for us (not kidding).

In acknowledgment, first and foremost, I'd like to thank Key West. It's a slice of paradise. Key West was my amusing Muse. That's probably why everyone on the island is, by law, a writer. Secondly, I'd like to thank my writing coach Lisa Mahoney. I'm so grateful for her encouragement, support and her ability to draw a mean story arc diagram. We laughed a lot, even when we weren't drinking. Thanks also to my husband Tom. I accepted 98 percent of his suggestions. Believe me, the other two percent were a better fit for a *different* genre of book.

Thank you to all of the wonderful pledgers, without whom this book would not have been possible. Many thanks to Unbound Publishing and their wonderful, professional staff across the pond. You are fabulous.

Patrons

John Kenney
Ashley Shields